BLOTTO, TWINKS
AND THE
RODENTS OF THE RIVIERA

BLOTTO, TWINKS AND THE RODENTS OF THE RIVIERA

Simon Brett

WINDSOR
PARAGON

First published 2011
by Constable
This Large Print edition published 2011
by AudioGO Ltd
by arrangement with
Constable & Robinson Ltd

Hardcover ISBN: 978 1 445 85844 9
Softcover   ISBN: 978 1 445 85845 6

British Library Cataloguing in Publication Data available

Printed and bound in Great Britain by
MPG Books Group Limited

To my goddaughter Elizabeth

1

Robbery at Tawcester Towers!

'Obviously, they're all portraits of our ancestors,' said Blotto, as he continued his guided tour of the Tawcester Towers Long Gallery. He chuckled. 'I mean, no one has pictures on their walls that aren't of their ancestors, do they?'

'I believe representations of other artistic subject matter have been observed on the walls of the middle classes,' replied the Marquis of Bluntleigh.

Blotto was impressed. 'Toad-in-the-hole, Buzzer!'

'And some of them even have reproductions.'

Blotto knew the word. It brought back rather embarrassing memories of a very red-faced chaplain at Eton explaining that babies weren't brought by storks or found under gooseberry bushes. He was confused. 'Sorry, Buzzer? Not with you. I'm afraid my touchpaper hasn't ignited yet.'

'The middle classes sometimes have pictures on their walls that are reproductions.'

'Pictures of people reproducing?'

'No, reproduction pictures,' the Marquis of Bluntleigh explained patiently. 'The middle classes sometimes have on their walls paintings that are not originals, but are printed copies of originals.'

'Broken biscuits,' said Blotto. 'I didn't know you could get pictures that weren't originals. How do you know guff like that, Buzzer?'

'When he was alive, my pater always encouraged me to mingle with the middle classes.'

'Well, I'll be snickered! Why on earth did the old fruitbat do that?'

'He said one never knew when one might want to borrow money from them.'

'Oh, I read your semaphore. Yes, good ticket. Few of us can avoid all contact with those banking oiks.' A shudder of distaste at the thought ran through every fibre of Blotto's aristocratic body. 'Now this is a portrait of the seventh Duke . . .'

More properly known as the Honourable Devereux Lyminster, younger son of the late Duke of Tawcester, Blotto was not enjoying himself. On such a crisp November morning, he would rather have been out hunting. In fact he would always rather be out hunting. And he'd certainly rather have been out hunting than entertaining the Marquis of Bluntleigh. But the Dowager Duchess had told him that that was his morning duty, and Blotto knew better than ever to question his mother's orders, however unappealing they might be.

It wasn't that Blotto had anything against the Marquis. The chap had also been at Eton, for a start, though a few years ahead, so obviously there were no worries about his gentlemanly credentials. Any Old Etonian was bound to be as straight as a six over the bowler's head.

And even though the Marquis's breeding wasn't quite all it should have been—his mother was French—he almost ranked as high as families who could date their ancestry back to the Norman Conquest. And, of course, when Blotto came to think of it, the boddos who came over with the Conqueror had originated in France too. So having a wealthy widowed mother who lived in a large château in the Midi was not such a social minus as it might at first appear. And, in fact, the Marquis of Bluntleigh's mother had had some kind of title in her own right (but a French one, so it didn't count for much).

The only other blemish on the Marquis's copybook was that, presumably because of his mother, he was a Catholic. Now Blotto had no animus against Catholics, he just felt sorry for the poor old thimbles. It wasn't only the permanent guilt that seemed to be an essential part of their religion, it was all that stuff they had to believe in. How much simpler, he thought, to be brought up like him—Church of England, which didn't involve believing in anything very much.

So Blotto had nothing against the Marquis, but the fact remained that the two of them had about as much in common as a revolver and a radish. For a start, the Marquis of Bluntleigh didn't like hunting. Almost worse, he didn't like cricket. Or even shooting. And as if those shortcomings weren't enough to snap the candle-snuffer on the prospect of any deep friendship between the two of them, he *did* apparently like books. Now, though Blotto had for some years been manfully working his way through *The Hand of Fu Manchu*, literature had never played a major part in his life. Tawcester Towers Library might have featured one of the most famous book collections in the British Isles but, in common with all his male predecessors, Blotto had never opened the leather-bound cover of any of them.

In this respect he was totally different from his sister, Lady Honoria Lyminster, known to everyone of her class (and of course, by definition,

3

she wasn't known to anyone who wasn't of her class) as Twinks. His sister, Blotto had known from an early age, was a Grade A brainbox, and it was a source of constant wonderment to him that such a Rolls-Royce of an intellect could fit inside so delicate a chassis.

Readily recognizing her superior intelligence and his own inadequacy in that department, he had never felt a moment's jealousy. In fact, he adored Twinks, but that particular November morning Blotto's admiration was diluted with a little resentment. It was her fault that he had got saddled with the Marquis of Bluntleigh.

Twinks, you see, had an unfortunate propensity for making men fall in love with her. And, remarkably, it wasn't her enormous intellect that attracted them. In fact, men in her circle wouldn't have recognized a woman's intellect until it came up and slapped them in the face—and in many cases, not even then. No, what translated every man who met her into an abjectly amorous swain was Twinks's beauty.

The combination of white-blond hair and azure eyes set in a complexion of rose-tinted ivory has always rendered males vulnerable. Add to these a perfect figure whose apparent fragility belied its considerable strength, a voice like the tinkling of a crystal chandelier, a laugh as teasing as a summer breeze, and you had in Twinks a walking man-trap.

The Marquis of Bluntleigh was only the latest in a long line of victims who had tumbled into its jaws.

But for Blotto he presented a new and rather worrying challenge. Though the Dowager Duchess had frequently expressed her intention to breed from her daughter, so far Twinks had been cunning enough to frustrate these plans. Her main objection to most of the extremely wealthy aristocrats lined up as potential husbands for her was their intellectual poverty. But of course that was of no concern to the Dowager Duchess.

The many criteria the old lady brought into her complex matrimonial calculations did not include a brain-cell count. The almost complete imbecility of the late Duke had not had any adverse effect on her own marriage—indeed in many ways may have improved it. And the inherited intellectual deficiency of his heir, the current Duke of Tawcester—known universally as Loofah—wasn't a problem in his marriage either. The only trouble there was his angular wife Sloggo's inability to produce any babies that weren't girls, thus raising the ghastly prospect of the dukedom devolving to some distant black-sheep cousin from Australia. Or, even worse in the view of the Dowager Duchess, to Blotto.

No, although a lot of minor qualifications had also to be met, the two essentials the Dowager Duchess demanded in a prospective suitor for her daughter were breeding and wealth. Brains didn't come into it.

The Marquis of Bluntleigh, however, did have quite a good brain. He had that slightly distracted air of someone in whose mind wheels were turning. Also, as already established, he liked books. Rumour even had it that he was an aspiring poet. These attributes made him, to Blotto's mind, a rather menacing figure.

Twinks was already showing more interest in Buzzer Bluntleigh than she had in any previous

5

besotted swain. This worried her brother on two counts. One, the idea of Twinks actually marrying threatened the charmed and unchanging idyll they both shared at Tawcester Towers. And, second, if the Dowager Duchess managed to get Twinks married off, there would be nothing to stop her focusing the full beam of her matrimonial energies on finding a bride for her younger son.

To Blotto, the prospect was appalling. He liked girls well enough, even enjoyed flirting a bit with some of his sister's friends. But there was a huge difference between a girl and a wife. Something happened to a woman when she got a wedding ring on her finger. He'd seen the ghastly consequences all too often with his schoolfriends. One moment they'd been carefree, *insouciant* idiots sploshing their way merrily through their inheritances, then suddenly overnight they'd be in thrall to some woman and taking seriously her suggestion that they didn't really need to open another bottle of claret. Blotto had even heard—unbelievable though the idea might be—of women who'd made their husbands give up hunting.

So he was in no hurry to engage with matrimony. Blotto was a great supporter of the status quo (or he would have been if he'd remembered the expression from his Latin lessons at Eton).

It was with mixed feelings therefore that he escorted the potentially dangerous Buzzer Bluntleigh through the Long Gallery of Tawcester Towers. And though *noblesse oblige* might have been an expression Blotto had forgotten from his French lessons at Eton, he understood its principle all right. The Marquis was a guest in the house and so, whatever designs he might have on Twinks, he must be accorded appropriate politeness.

'Now this . . .' a gesture to another portrait, 'is the high-spending fifth Duke, known as "Black Rupert" . . . his son the equally irresponsible sixth Duke, known as "Rupert the Fiend" . . . and this one's his son whose success in restoring the financial stability of Tawcester Towers earned him the nickname of "Rupert the Dull".'

'Rupert a bit of a family name for you, is it?' asked Buzzer Bluntleigh, raising the comforting hope in Blotto that perhaps his intellect wasn't all it had been cracked up to be. And the comforting possibility that this might make the Marquis less attractive to Twinks.

He confirmed the self-evident truth. 'With the Tawcesters the eldest son's always a Rupert. Second son's always a Devereux.'

'And what about further sons?'

This was another encouraging indication of Buzzer Bluntleigh's stupidity. 'There aren't any further sons,' Blotto explained patiently. 'Just me and Loofah. Oh, and Twinks obviously. But she's not a son, she's a daughter.'

'I am well aware of that.' A disturbingly soupy look came into the Marquis's eyes. 'And what a beautiful daughter.'

Blotto was momentarily tempted to start listing his sister's faults with a view to dampening this dangerous ardour, but he realized that would be disloyal. Besides, when he came to think of it, Twinks actually hadn't got any faults. No, he was going to have to find another way of sabotaging Buzzer Bluntleigh's matrimonial ambitions.

In the meantime, his guided tour had to continue. He gestured wearily up to the panelled wall. 'And here we have the sixth Duke and the seventh Duke, known respectively as "Rupert the Smug" and "Rupert the Incapable".'

'Where?' asked the Marquis of Bluntleigh.

'Well, *there*.' Rather petulantly Blotto repeated his gesture. But the look in Buzzer's eyes made him turn to look where he was pointing.

On the wall were two rectangular shapes, darker than the surrounding sun-bleached panelling, their outlines defined by dusty cobwebs. High up in the middle of each empty space, picture hooks poked out pathetically.

Rupert the Smug and Rupert the Incapable had been stolen!

2

Enter Twinks

Blotto should have realized that, having announced he was off to fetch his sister, he would inevitably find the Marquis of Bluntleigh still waiting in the Long Gallery on their return. The poor droplet was so besotted with Twinks that, for a glimpse of her, he would have waited forty-eight hours in his jim-jams under a leaking drainpipe. And indeed when she appeared, Buzzer Bluntleigh's jaw dropped down to near sock-suspender level, and his eyes took on the qualities of nearly hatched frogspawn.

She did, even her brother noticed, look particularly breathsapping that morning. The dress of silver-grey silk that encased her stopped just above the knee, revealing an enticement of silk-stockinged leg. A string of pearls dangled down almost to the hem of her dress, and nonchalantly from her wrist hung a silver-sequinned reticule.

The Marquis of Bluntleigh's jaw dropped further as it took in her loveliness. 'Um, er . . . um, er . . . um,' was the nearest he got to speech.

'So what have we here?' asked Twinks.

Blotto felt a sudden pang in his heart. He didn't think he'd ever had a pang before, and if that was what they felt like, then he didn't want any more of them. But the cause of this particular pang was his sister's use of the word 'we'. Could it be possible that she was including the Marquis of Bluntleigh in that all-enveloping pronoun? Was it conceivable that this incomer might not only steal Twinks away in marriage, but might also hope to share in the brother and sister's sleuthing activities? Just spelling out the question in his mind gave Blotto another pang.

Suppressing it, he tried not to show there was anything wrong as he replied to her question. 'It's not so much what's here, Twinks me old muffin—it's what isn't here.' And he directed her attention to the gaps on the wall.

'Great whiffling water rats!' she responded. 'There's been some sneaky backdoor-sidling going on here. We must find the stenchers who've done this!'

Another pang. Blotto tried desperately to remember whether his sister had ever talked so openly about a potential investigation with a third person present. Was she really considering turning their precious duo into a sleuthing trio?

But even as he had the thought, his fears were

allayed. Turning on her goldfish-mouthed swain a smile that could not fail to sink him deeper into the morass of his love, Twinks asked sweetly, 'Haven't you got anything you should be doing, Buzzer?'

'Er . . . what kind of thing?' he managed to reply.

Blotto was sympathetic to the Marquis's confusion. His sister's question was a really tricky one. Was there anything that someone of their class *should* be doing? Particularly if that someone didn't like hunting . . . or cricket . . . or shooting. Bit early in the day to be settling down in the billiard room with a decanter of brandy. No doubt about it, what Twinks had asked was a real stumper.

'Well, erm . . . anything, really,' she replied in an atypically feeble manner. She too must have been realizing the extent of the dilemma she had raised for her prospective fiancé.

But Twinks was never defeated for long. Her brother had seen her get out of much worse gluepots than this, so he was entirely unsurprised when she turned another ensnaring smile on the Marquis and said, 'You told me you were a poet, Buzzer . . .'

'Ah, well, um, er . . .'

'Why don't you go off and write a poem?'

'I . . . er . . . um . . .'

'For me.'

Of course that clinched it. Whether the ugly rumour about the Marquis being a poet was true or not, it was one that he had volunteered to Twinks, and now that she'd asked him specifically to write something for her, his bluff had been called. Blotto watched gleefully as Buzzer

Bluntleigh left the Long Gallery in search of quill pen and papyrus or whatever else it was that poets used in the plying of their unholy trade.

Twinks seemed as happy as he was at the departure of her amorous swain, so Blotto didn't even raise with her the question that had been troubling him. Twinks wouldn't play him a diddler's hand. Brother and sister were a team; it was unthinkable that anyone else would ever take a major part in one of their investigations.

He was relieved to see that Twinks didn't even cast a lovelorn eye towards her swain's retreating back. She seemed, encouragingly, to have forgotten all about the Marquis the moment he was out of her sight. And all she was interested in was the case in hand. Which realization was, for Blotto, all creamy éclair.

His sister's azure eyes sparkled as they looked up at the wall and focused on the two rectangles of darker wood. 'Our thieves knew what they were looking for,' she announced. 'Gainsborough and Reynolds!'

'Well, kipper me with a fish knife!' said her brother in awestruck tones. 'You absolutely are the lark's larynx, Twinks. Just one look at the wall and you know the names of the stenchers who snaffled the Ruperts.'

The pale skin of Twinks's forehead wrinkled in puzzlement. 'Not on the same page, Blotto me old trouser-button . . . ?'

'Well, you've bonged it on the nose first bash, haven't you? All we need to do is track down these two bad tomatoes called Gainsborough and Reynolds and the case'll be sewn up as neat as a Frenchwoman's facelift!'

11

'Um, no, Blotto,' said his sister gently. 'Gainsborough and Reynolds aren't the names of the thieves.'

'Then who are they? Their accomplices?'

'They're the painters. Thomas Gainsborough painted Rupert the Smug and Joshua Reynolds painted Rupert the Incapable.'

'Oh,' said Blotto, trying to make it the kind of 'Oh' that could mean 'Of course I knew that, Twinks me old tea-caddy—I was just having a bit of a jape with you.'

Evidently unaware of this subtext, Twinks tapped a pensive finger against her perfect chin. 'As I say, they knew what they were after. The Gainsborough and Reynolds are the only two really valuable paintings in the house.'

'Oh, so they only painted the two, did they?' Her brother gestured towards the Long Gallery's residual display. 'Got in other boddos to do the rest, did they?'

Once again his sister was very patient. 'Blotto, all of these paintings are of dukes, aren't they . . . ?'

'Yes. Our ancestors.'

'And the dukes all lived at different periods of history . . .'

'Right.'

'And you didn't have more than one duke at the same time . . .'

'I spoffing well hope you didn't.'

'So they would have had to be painted by different artists.'

Blotto still looked puzzled.

In a tone as near to exasperation as she ever got with her brother, Twinks explained, 'Gainsborough and Reynolds wouldn't have been alive to paint most of them, would they?'

'Ah, no. With you. Touchpaper ignited,' said Blotto finally. 'So when it comes to art, these two Gainsborough and Reynolds boddos are the chef's speciality, are they?'

'With dollops of clotted cream, Blotto me old trombone. Those two paintings the stenchers got away with are each worth hundreds of thous.'

He emitted an impressed whistle. 'Well, I'll be jugged like a hare! What kind of pot-brained pineapple would want to collect pictures of our ancestors?'

'I think,' said Twinks gently, 'it's the painters rather than their subjects that provide the value.'

'That's a bit of a rum baba. I mean, this pair of greengages Gainsborough and Reynolds weren't titled, were they?'

'Joshua Reynolds was knighted by George III in 1769.'

'Twinks me old collar-stud, I was talking about proper titles. Any jumped-up town councillor can buy a knighthood. Or a peerage these days, come to that. You should hear Loofah on the subject. Some of these life peers he has to rub shoulders with in the House of Lords are total toadspawn.'

But Twinks did not want at that moment to be diverted by discussion of the views of their brother the Duke. 'Blotto, we shouldn't waste time gabbing. We need to track down the four-faced filchers who've snaffled our paintings.'

'Good ticket, Twinks. But how are we going to do that?'

'Just give me a minute.'

3

Twinks Brings Her Brain to Bear

Blotto was reverentially silent. His respect for his sister was total in every area of life, but particularly in the matter of criminal investigation. When it came to spotting clues, Twinks had sharper eyes than the mother of an unmarried son at a coming-out ball. So her brother watched in awe as her mighty intellect was focused on the section of wall where Rupert the Smug and Rupert the Incapable had so recently hung.

There was a silence almost as long as the gallery, while the azure eyes flicked from point to point, reading from the wooden surface information invisible to the average scrutineer. And certainly to her brother.

Then Twinks exhaled a long, satisfied sigh, before confidently announcing, 'I think I see what happened.'

'Do you? Well, I'm snickered if I know how.'

'Just observation, Blotto. Look . . .' And she embarked on another of her remarkable explanations.

'As I said, the fact that they only took the Gainsborough and the Reynolds means that we are dealing with educated and discriminating thieves. They knew what they wanted, they knew where they'd find it, and so the stenchers must've put in a lot of planning. Security here at Tawcester Towers is always pretty lax, so they wouldn't have had much trouble getting in. But if they'd been dressed

14

as servants, there was a real danger that they'd be seen by other members of staff who'd realize they didn't match the wallpaper. So I'd bet a banjo to a banana that our thieves were guests here at Tawcester Towers.'

Blotto was shocked. 'What, you mean people of our class?'

'Well, people who've been invited here for a weekend. Some of those,' she pointed out tactfully, 'are not exactly of our class.'

'You've won a coconut there, Twinks me old fondant fancy. All kinds of oikish sponge-worms seem to turn up at weekends. Do you know, Loofah actually told me he was out shooting on the estate a couple of weeks back and he found the gun next to him was a solicitor! Toad-in-the-hole, what's going on in this country, when tradesmen like that manage to get invited here?'

'What you're saying rather reinforces my point, Blotto me old trouser turn-up. It'd be as easy as raspberries for the thieves to get in. I mean, do you notice exactly who all our guests are every weekend?'

'Great Wilberforce, no. Of course I don't. I mean, I'm polite to the poor thimbles, but I never know their names or any of that rombooley.'

'Then I'm sure the theft of the Gainsborough and the Reynolds happened last weekend. You remember how many people we had staying then?'

'Certainly do. Tawcester Towers was doing a fair impression of Piccadilly Circus. Breakfast on Sunday morning I recall was like a particularly vigorous Eton Wall Game.'

'And can you remember any of the guests behaving oddly?'

15

'Well, they were all behaving pretty oddly, I thought. Mind you, I think most people do behave pretty oddly most of the time. Except for the immediate family, obviously. And, actually, now I come to think of it, Loofah has his behaving-oddly moments.'

The smooth skin around Twinks's eyes wrinkled with the effort of recollection. Then she announced, 'There was one particular pair of guests who, now I come to think of it, stuck out like slugs in a salad.'

'Oh?'

'Do you remember the French couple?' Blotto's handsome face retained its customary blankness, so Twinks gave his memory a nudge. 'The Vicomte and Vicomtesse de Sales-Malincourt. There was something about them that didn't pluck the right string with me.'

'Well, of course they didn't pluck the right string—they were French. What did you expect? The poor pineapples started off on the back foot and had a lot of ground to make up.' A look of deep compassion spread across Blotto's patrician features. 'I can never begin to understand how foreigners cope with knowing that they're not British. Must wake up every morning aware that they're in the deepest gluepot. And then those two calling themselves aristocrats—that was rich! The French aristocracy doesn't amount to an empty soup plate.'

'Because of the French Revolution, you mean?'

'No. They didn't amount to an empty soup plate before that. They've never had a proper aristocracy. Not like ours. I mean, the English aristocracy has always been the genuine article,

16

but—'

'Blotto!'

So sudden was his sister's shouting out his name that he was momentarily anxious. 'You all right, old kipper?'

'I've just remembered something.' An azure flame of excitement flickered in Twinks's eyes. 'You know everyone went hunting on Saturday morning?'

'Yes, of course I do.'

'Well, everyone didn't.'

'Sorry? Not on the same page, Twinks.'

'The Vicomte and Vicomtesse de Sales-Malincourt didn't go hunting on Saturday morning.'

'Rather proves my point about the French, I'd have said.'

'She said she had a bit of a head cold, and the Vicomte volunteered to stay in the house to keep her company.'

To Blotto this was just more evidence of the perils of the marital state. For a man to give up a day's hunting just because his wife had a head cold ... well, if that didn't take the pink rosette! Should that kind of nonsense take hold, next thing men'd be stopped from dining at their clubs just because their wives were having babies.

But he didn't voice his thoughts. Twinks was on a roll, and he knew better than to offer any distraction when the engine of her mighty brain was building up a head of steam. So Blotto just listened as she went on, 'I'd put my last crumb of rock cake on the fact that the job was done on Saturday morning. And I bet no one's been in the Long Gallery since then.'

17

'Probably not. I don't think any of the weekend guests were interested in art. Or our ancestors, come to that.'

'No.' Twinks tapped her chin reflectively. 'So . . . our thieves . . . I wonder who they are.'

It wasn't often that Blotto could get one up on his sister, so he wasn't about to waste the opportunity. 'I'm surprised you've forgotten so fast,' he said gleefully. 'They're the Vicomte and Vicomtesse de Sales-Malincourt.'

'Yes,' agreed Twinks, dashing his hopes of triumph, 'but who are they *really*?'

Blotto couldn't come up with an answer to that one.

'I'm sure they were in disguise,' his sister went on, 'though their French was very good, so I think they were born French-speakers. But the two main questions we have to answer are: Who are they? And where are they now?'

Blotto didn't venture an opinion. He just watched reverently as the delicate mechanism of Twinks's brain processed the available information.

'I'm certain they'll have left some more clues here,' she said, and reached into her sequinned reticule to produce a silver-handled magnifying glass. 'Let's just see what's what.' She moved closer to the exposed panelling and began to trace the cobwebbed outlines of the missing Gainsborough and Reynolds. 'Nobody ever goes anywhere without leaving some souvenirs of their presence. For the amateur sleuth the skill lies in reading the messages that have been posted for us.'

Her scrutiny of the crime scene took two long, silent minutes. Then, with a triumphant smile,

18

Twinks turned to her brother and announced, 'It is very clear what happened.'

'Is it?'

'Oh yes. Cobwebs are wonderful devices for storing evidence, you know. They're as sticky as Belgian caramel. And these ones from behind the picture frames have trapped plenty of clues. Our filth-fingering thieves have given us directions as clear as the road-sign to the new A1. They couldn't have made our task easier if they'd presented us with calling cards. Look, Blotto . . .'

A slender finger pointed out her findings as she itemized them. 'Obviously the stenchers wore gloves. They knew better than to risk leaving fingerprints. But they did leave other traces.' The finger homed in on a tiny pinkish fleck on one of the cobwebs. 'See? That comes from a lady's kid glove. Not just any kid glove either. If I'm not mistaken—'

'And of course you never are, Twinks.'

'No,' she acknowledged gracefully. 'Anyway, I'd say it's forty thou to a fishbone that these gloves were bought from Maison Grière in the Rue du Faubourg Saint-Michel in Paris.'

'Toad-in-the-hole!'

'So we know where the so-called Vicomtesse de Sales-Malincourt does her shopping. Not quite Champs-Élysées style—in fact the kind of place where tradesmen's wives might shop. Now here . . .' the finger moved to another area of cobweb, 'we see the marks left by her husband—or probably the bad tomato who was masquerading as her husband. From his glove came this tiny flake of tobacco.' Twinks advanced her delicate nose to the wall and sniffed. 'Which, if I'm not very much mistaken . . .'

Blotto didn't bother repeating how rarely that eventuality occurred. They both knew, anyway.

'. . . comes from a cheap cigar imported from Bolivia and sold only in a small *tabac* on the Rue des Folies-de-Grandeur in Paris. You're beginning to see a pattern emerging here, aren't you, Blotto?'

Her brother was forced to admit that he wasn't.

'Well, let's look at the third piece of evidence, the clincher, the cherry on the top of my investigative *meringue glacé* . . .' This time she redirected her finger from the wall to the Long Gallery's oak flooring, worn smooth by generations of peers' slippers and housemaids' mops. 'Do you see that outline there?'

Blotto couldn't see anything but he didn't want to stop his sister in mid-flow, so he nodded vigorously.

'That very slight indentation in the wood shows that a heavy object has rested there. Given the angle and depth of the indentation, I have no doubt in announcing that it was made by the brass corner of a custom-built carrying case for ladies' dresses, manufactured in the *atelier* of Honoré Dumartin in Neuilly-sur-Seine on the outskirts of Paris and sold exclusively in Galeries Pfitzer in Avenue Laliquette. Interesting, isn't it, Blotto me old ham sandwich?'

He couldn't deny that it was indeed interesting. Though why he hadn't a clue.

'And particularly interesting because of where the purchases were made. Maison Grière and the *tabac* on the Rue des Folies-de-Grandeur both cater for people who work for their living . . .'

'Oikish riff-raff you mean?'

'Precisely. Whereas Galeries Pfitzer in Avenue Laliquette is very much top leaf on the family tree. So why should this couple of Grade Z filchers suddenly be shopping there?'

'Why, indeed?'

'Because, Blotto, what they bought in Galeries Pfitzer is one of the most important parts of their professional equipment.'

'Oh?'

'Look, if you're masquerading as members of the aristocracy . . .'

'Only the French aristocracy,' Blotto pointed out.

'Even so. If you're claiming a title to which you have no right and snaffling invitations to country houses, what's the one thing that's going to show you up?'

At last—a question to which Blotto knew the answer. 'Your luggage.'

'Bong on the nose, Blotto. If you turned up with tonky luggage, the servants'd be on to you straight away. Doesn't matter how old your valises are—indeed the older and more decrepit the better . . . *so long as they were bought at the right place.*'

Her brother nodded agreement. Twinks looked down again at the floor. 'Judging from the depth of this indentation, the carrying case would have been about a foot deep, three foot across the bottom and five in height. Perfect for hanging ladies' dresses in . . . and also perfect for . . . ?'

'Storing your cricket bats?' hazarded Blotto.

'Possibly,' said his sister kindly. 'But something of that size would also be perfect for . . . hiding stolen paintings.'

Her brother grinned. 'On the same page with you

now, Twinks.'

'And when the filchers left, they'd have actually got the Tawcester Towers servants to carry their loot out of the house.'

'The deceitful lumps of toadspawn! How're we going to find the slimy spongebags?'

'Ah, well, there I'd say they've made the job very easy for us.'

'Have they?'

'It's a simple matter of geographical triangulation.'

'Well, I'll be crackered.'

'Visualize the map of Paris . . .' Blotto furrowed his brow, as if he was following his sister's request. Despite the fact that he couldn't even visualise the map of his own bedroom. '. . . and it all becomes clear,' Twinks went on. 'Rue du Faubourg Saint-Michel . . . Rue des Folies-de-Grandeur . . . Avenue Laliquette . . . Three streets in the Cinquième Arrondissement that form a triangle in the middle of which is La Place Biscuit de Garibaldi. As we know, the north and east sides of the square are government offices. On the west side is the Convent of Les Petites Amies de Dieu. But on the south side we have a residential building called Les Appartements Clichy. The block is four storeys high, with two mansion flats on each floor. The numbering of the residences starts on the ground floor. Now, no thieves would ever take an upstairs apartment if they could avoid it. They might get trapped up there if they were raided by the police. So they'd want to be at street level. There are two apartments at street level, but the one on the west side gets so much afternoon sun that it could damage the paintings that are stored there before being sold on.

'So I can confidently state that the address of the so-called Vicomte and Vicomtesse de Sales-Malincourt is Appartement 2, Les Appartements Clichy, Place Biscuit de Garibaldi, Cinquième Arrondissement, Paris.'

'France,' added Blotto, feeling that he ought to make a contribution to his sister's research.

4

A Matter of Insurance

'Insurance?' echoed the Dowager Duchess magisterially. 'But that's for common people.'

'Are you telling us, mater,' asked Blotto, 'that nothing in Tawcester Towers is insured?'

They were sitting in the Blue Morning Room. This was where, from a splendid Chippendale throne, the Dowager Duchess traditionally conducted her business affairs. At his question, she turned a full beam of disapproval on to her younger son. 'Of course not. To resort to insurance would not be in keeping with the hallowed traditions of the Tawcester family. For a start, it would involve sullying our hands by dealing with members of the oikish classes like solicitors and another sub-species of pond life who I believe are referred to as . . .' she shuddered with distaste, '"insurance brokers". Then again, to insure one's valuables goes against the very traditions of the aristocracy. It implies that one does not trust the people whom one has invited into one's home. It suggests that one might suspect one's own guests of being capable of larceny.'

'But in this case,' Twinks pointed out, 'some of our guests *have* proved capable of larceny.'

'Then it was our error,' the Dowager Duchess announced, 'for inviting such people. And to make a claim on insurance would be a public admission of that error.'

'Except, of course,' said her son, 'since nothing's insured, we couldn't make a claim on insurance, anyway.'

'That is not the point, Blotto. The issue is one of standards. Standards by which people of our sort have conducted themselves across the centuries. Stealing from each other has long been a tradition of the British upper classes. The expression "robber baron" did not come about by accident. Sacking and pillaging each other's homes is an aristocratic pastime going back almost to pre-history. And if a nobleman's castle was pillaged during, let us say, the Wars of the Roses, he did not seek reparation from an insurance company.'

'So how did he seek reparation?' asked Blotto, a trifle nervously.

'He sought reparation by pillaging the castle of the nobleman who'd pillaged his. In this way valuables were kept circulating among the right people.'

'But, Mater,' asked Twinks, 'are you suggesting that we do nothing about the theft of the paintings? That we just let the stenchers get away with it?'

'Of course I'm not suggesting that,' the Dowager Duchess rumbled like a volcano contemplating eruption. 'The Vicomte and Vicomtesse de Sales-

Malincourt have impugned the honour of the Tawcester family. What is more, they have offended against all traditional codes of hospitality. They have behaved exactly in the manner that one would have expected of French aristocrats.'

'Though, in fact,' said Twinks, 'we have pretty strong reasons to suspect that they aren't aristocrats, anyway.'

'That's what I said. French aristocrats aren't proper aristocrats.'

'No. But we believe that those two lumps of toadspawn were *pretending* to be members of the French aristocracy.'

'What a bizarre thing to want to pretend to be.'

'Not,' Twinks pointed out, 'if you want to snaffle an invitation to a weekend house party with a view to filching a Gainsborough and a Reynolds.'

Grumpily, the Dowager Duchess conceded that her daughter had a point. 'The important thing,' she said, 'is what we now do about what's happened.'

'The answer to that's obvious, Mater.'

'Is it?'

'Is it?' echoed Blotto, as ever having a little difficulty keeping up with his sister's thought processes.

'We get the Gainsborough and the Reynolds back,' announced Twinks.

'And how do you achieve that?'

'We go to France.'

'And who is "we", may I ask?'

'Blotto, me, with Corky Froggett to drive us.'

'Hm . . .' The Dowager Duchess's complexion turned a deeper shade of mauve as she contemplated this suggestion. 'The fact is, Honoria, I am not sure that you can be spared at this time. Your presence is required here at Tawcester Towers.'

'Why, Mater?'

'It may not have escaped your notice that the Marquis of Bluntleigh is here as a long-term guest ...'

Oh, broken biscuits, thought Blotto. The mater was still pursuing her plan of breeding from Twinks and Buzzer Bluntleigh. That was a real stye in the eye. Once the Dowager Duchess got her teeth into an idea, her grip was like that of a Staffordshire bull terrier. And the similarities between the two species didn't end there.

Fortunately, as ever, Twinks had her arguments well marshalled. 'Mater, you want the Gainsborough and the Reynolds back, don't you?' The Dowager Duchess could not deny that she did. 'Which means that someone's got to go to France to get them back. Now obviously the job can't be done by anyone outside the family. Otherwise the news of theft would soon spread abroad and the Tawcesters would become a laughing stock. Well, Loofah can't go and tangle with these four-faced French filchers, can he?'

'It would not befit his ducal position.'

'Bong on the nose, Mater. So the two remaining possibilities are ... that Blotto and I go together, as suggested ... or that Blotto goes to sort the thing out on his own?'

There was no contest. The Dowager Duchess was a woman of few illusions, and she certainly entertained none about the intellectual capacity of her younger son. It was agreed that Blotto and

26

Twinks should both go to France to rescue the stolen Ruperts. And they both felt confident they could sort out that little mission and still be back at Tawcester Towers in time for Christmas.

*   *   *

Lingering outside the Blue Morning Room stood the Marquis of Bluntleigh. From his face hung the gloopy lovelorn expression of a stage-door Johnnie. But it was no chorus girl for whom he waited. It was Twinks.

As soon as she and Blotto emerged from the audience with their mother, the Marquis stepped forward, his Adam's apple bobbling like a ping-pong ball on a fairground fountain. He thrust into his beloved's hand a folded sheet of thick writing paper. 'This is for you,' he managed to articulate, before scurrying off down the corridor like a hare with an upset stomach.

Twinks invited her brother up to the boudoir adjacent to her bedroom to plan their forthcoming trip. Once there she offered him a cup of cocoa and when he accepted, amazingly, she didn't ring for a maid to make it. Instead she switched on the electric ring and prepared the drink herself. Blotto was sometimes quite shocked by his sister's modern ways.

While the milk was boiling, there was a knock on the boudoir door and on Twinks's command Grimshaw, the Tawcester Towers butler, entered with a thick letter on a silver salver. 'I'm sorry to trouble you, milady, but this has just arrived by special delivery. I was told you were expecting it.'

'Oh, larksissimo! Good ticket, Grimshaw. You

27

may go.'

The minute the butler was out of the door, Twinks had the stout manila envelope open and was scanning its contents.

'What's the bizz-buzz?' asked Blotto.

'From Razzy.'

He looked puzzled. 'Not on the same page, Twinks me old prawn sandwich.'

'Razzy. Professor Erasmus Holofernes. You know—don.'

'Don? I thought you said he was called Razzy.'

'No, he is a don. At St Raphael's College, Oxford. I've often talked about him. He's helped me with research on a few cases.'

'Oh.' There was a slight frostiness in Blotto's tone. He did remember Holofernes now. A man with a machine-like brain that could instantly process volumes of information. And though Blotto was modest enough to recognize that he himself could never bring that kind of intellect to bear on a problem, he still resented Twinks's recourse to anyone else when they were conducting an investigation. Blotto liked things better when it was just the two of them.

But he couldn't help being caught up in her excitement as Twinks cried, 'Oh, this is jollissimo! Look what Razzy's found for us!'

Her use of the word 'us' rather than 'me' immediately thawed any residual frost in Blotto. While Twinks perused the thick file from the package, he looked at the photographs she had passed over to him. Both featured a man and a woman. In one they were dressed in the style of the last Emperor and Empress of Russia before things got rather uncomfortable for them. In the

28

next they wore the clothes of a London Pearly King and Queen.

'Who are these four people?' asked Blotto.

'There are only two of them,' replied Twinks without looking up from her reading.

It was rarely that her brother could score points off her so easily. 'I'm sorry, Twinks me old sheet of blotting paper. There are four—two in each photograph. So snubbins to you!'

'Blotto me old tinkling sackbut, it's the same people in both pics. According to Razzy, they are a pair of international jewel thieves. They are both French. Nobody knows their real names, but of course you and I know them as . . . ?'

This was too tough a question for Blotto. His brow corrugated like cardboard.

As ever, his sister helped him out. 'These two are the ones we know as the Vicomte and Vicomtesse de Sales-Malincourt.'

'Toad-in-the-hole,' murmured Blotto. 'They look entirely different in each photograph.'

'That is because they are masters of disguise. According to Razzy, they're famous for it. They once snaffled the Contessa del Biagio's sapphires disguised as chimney sweeps.'

'That was spoffing clever . . .'

'It was indeed.'

'. . . to think of disguising sapphires as chimney sweeps.'

'No, Blotters, what I meant was . . .' But Twinks didn't pursue it. 'Yes, they are masters of disguise, but we can still always recognize the stenchers.'

'Can we?'

'Yes. Don't you see on these photographs? They both have distinctive features that cannot be hidden by any amount of greasepaint or drapery.'

Blotto looked hard. He couldn't see anything. 'Do they?'

'Yes. There—there is a mole on the woman's chin, slightly to the right of centre. And there again—the man has a scar high on his left cheekbone. Don't forget those details, Blotto me old shove-ha'penny board. They could be very significant when we get to Paris.'

'I'll remember them. A mole and a scar.' He nodded his head as he assimilated the information.

'You're sure that's nailed firmly to the interior of your brainbox, Blotters?' Twinks asked with the maximum of tact. There had been occasions during previous investigations when she had found her brother's memory wanting. Though he could remember each moment of every day's hunting he'd ever participated in, his bag for every day's shooting and the details of every cricket match recorded in *Wisden*, Blotto was less of a whale on those secret codes and minutiae of clues which were so essential to the business of detection.

'Don't worry. Mole on the right of the woman's chin—scar on the man's left cheekbone. Knowing that kind of guff, we'll track down the stenchers.'

'Of course we will, Blotters!' She put down the file and turned on her brother a smile of sheer devilment. 'Pure creamy éclair for us to be involved in another investigation, isn't it?'

'It's absolutely the lark's larynx, Twinks me old tin tray.'

During their perusal of Professor Holofernes's research the milk had gone cold, but Twinks reboiled it and made their promised cocoa. When they were sitting sipping in blissful togetherness,

Blotto noticed, fallen on the floor, the missive that the Marquis of Bluntleigh had given to his sister. 'Going to check the SP on that? Might be another clue, eh?'

Twinks picked up the paper and perused its contents. After a moment she sighed. 'Oh dear, Blotters. I'm afraid Buzzer's written me a poem.'

'Well, you did ask him to.'

'Yes, but I never thought he'd take the idea off the starting blocks. Still, I suppose it's flattering for a girl to be a muse.'

'To be a mews?'

'Yes, Blotto.'

'But how can a girl be a mews? I mean, a mews is a sort of stable block and—'

'I think we're talking about a different kind of muse, Blotto.'

'Oh?'

'A muse can be a woman who inspires art. Like Beatrice for Dante or Laura for Petrarch.'

Blotto shook his head. 'Don't think I've met any of those boddos.'

'No, you wouldn't have done. They lived a long time ago.'

'Ah.'

'But wouldn't it be larksissimo for a girl to be someone's muse? To be the inspiration for a great work of art, to live immortalised in that work of art.'

Blotto didn't like the animated glow that this thought brought to his sister's cheeks. Once again he felt a stab of jealousy. Maybe the Marquis of Bluntleigh wasn't the vacuum-brain he appeared to be? Maybe he really had found the way to snaffle the heart of the Honourable Honoria

Lyminster? Blotto watched with anxiety as Twinks read the handwritten lines.

There was a long silence after she'd finished reading, a silence in which Blotto hung nervously. Then, to his enormous relief, Twinks thrust the paper into his hands with a cheery cry of: 'What absolute guff!'

'You mean it's not great art?'

'If that's great art I'm an Apache dancer. It's total toffee from top to tail. Go on, read it.'

'But surely, Twinks, if it's meant for you . . . I don't want to be snibbing in someone else's back yard.'

'You won't be. Go on, read it.'

'I'm not much of a whale on poetry. I—'

'For the love of strawberries, read it!'

Blotto did as he was told. The Marquis of Bluntleigh's poem ran thus:

> *How beautiful you are, you really set me on*
> *   fire—*
> *Though what I feel for you is a very*
> *   respectable and honourable desire,*
> *Not the kind of thing that your mother or any*
> *   other relative need worry about,*
> *But I really do want to know whether I'm in*
> *   with a shout*
> *Of ending up as your husband, that is to say*
> *   with you as my wife,*
> *Because I think we could make a fair fist of*
> *   things if we shared together our life.*
> *There are lots of arguments in favour of such*
> *   a thing happening,*
> *And if it did I would jolly well sing.*
> *You're beautiful, as I said before in this poem,*

32

a lovely lass,
And we both belong to the same class,
Which means us getting married would be
*   extremely suitable*
And, as I said before in this poem, you're
*   beautiful.*
Also I'm extremely well heeled with not just a
*   title but a lot of family loot too,*
Not just some parvenu.
Twinks, you make every one of my jolly old
*   nerve-ends tingle*
And you're the reason why I don't want to
*   end up as a mournful old man staying*
*   single.*

Now, by his own admission, Blotto didn't know much about poetry. But he looked up from the page with an expression of delighted relief. Even someone with a knowledge of poetry as limited as his could recognize bilge-water when he saw it. The threat of the Marquis of Bluntleigh stealing away his sister seemed suddenly to have diminished.

5

To France!

The crossing to France was rough and they were glad that the Lagonda had been lashed down firmly on to the ferry's deck. Blotto was also glad that safely in one of his valises in the car was his favourite cricket bat. He wasn't optimistic of finding a game across the Channel. He knew the French were a degenerate lot whose only idea of sport was pongling around on push-bikes, but he always felt reassured to know the bat was in his luggage. Blotto had a ritual of stroking the battered willow last thing at night and the familiar whiff of linseed oil always wafted him into dreamless sleep.

During the crossing Twinks entertained herself lying on a bunk and reading Sun Tzu's *The Art of War* in the original Chinese, while her brother and Corky Froggett bought each other an unending sequence of brandies in the ship's bar.

'The thing is, milord,' the chauffeur pontificated, his moustache and hair bristling, 'that the French have never had any guts. They showed that during the last big dust-up. Just rolled over and let the Jerries trample all over 'em. Then we had to come in and sort things out for them. It's all that fancified food they eat. Give 'em some boiled beef and carrots—that'd sort 'em out.'

It went against Blotto's sense of fair play to criticize anyone, but he couldn't help feeling a sneaking sympathy for what Corky Froggett was saying. He had nothing against the French, all he felt for them was pity. They did make life unnecessarily complicated for themselves. And it wasn't just their food. All that rombooley about driving on the wrong side of the road—where did that idea come from? And then making tiny nippers learn French at such an early age . . . That was hardly fair on the poor little squibs, was it? How much easier it would be for them if they did the natural thing and learned English.

Meanwhile Corky Froggett was chuntering on.

'Didn't feel right, milord, you know, when I was over here fighting the Jerries on the same side as the French. They're our natural enemies, the French are, have been through history. Now if it had been us against the Germans *and* the French, well, that would have made a lot more sense. And the odds would have been fairer. We'd still have won, and all. I'm a finely tuned killing machine, you know, milord, and it really went against my instincts not being allowed to kill any of the French . . .'

Blotto had always recognized that Corky Froggett had a tendency towards the homicidal. But at least his heart was in the right place.

*   *   *

Once they had checked into their suite at the Hôtel de Crillon, Twinks immediately telephoned Dimpsy Wickett-Coote, a schoolfriend who was currently living in Paris (and also, according to the old girls' bush telegraph, in sin). The two girls had met as twelve-year-olds at St Wilhelmina's Convent. (Up until that point Twinks had been educated by governesses at Tawcester Towers, but it was the view of her mother that she needed to mix with other 'gels'. And though the Dowager Duchess despised Catholicism, preferring the relaxed uncertainties of the Church of England, she approved of the discipline that nuns imposed on their charges.)

At St Wilhelmina's there had been an instant rapport between the two girls. Dimpsy wasn't as intelligent as Twinks (but then no one in the entire history of the known universe was as intelligent as

Twinks), but she shared with her a lively curiosity about the world, and an unwillingness to toe the line of convention.

Nor did Dimpsy's breeding quite match up to her friend's. Indeed until his purchase of a peerage from the Lloyd George government, her father had been a mere Mr Wickett-Coote. But Twinks did not allow such considerations to affect her, and though obviously she didn't treat Dimpsy as an equal, she was happy to regard her as a co-conspirator. The escapades of the pair, and their ongoing war of attrition against the nuns, could have filled many volumes of school stories.

They left St Wilhelmina's at the age of eighteen, both lucky to make it that long, given the number of times the Mother Superior had threatened to expel them. Thereafter their paths had diverged, Twinks making her base at Tawcester Towers and concentrating on the investigation of murders, while Dimpsy moved to London and devoted her life to shocking her parents by linking up with a series of ever more unsuitable men. As a result, the two had met little in the previous few years—in fact, when Twinks came to think of it, only twice, at each other's coming-out balls—but their friendship had been maintained by a constant exchange of near-hysterical letters, written in a private slang incomprehensible to any but the participants (and sometimes not even to them).

When Twinks rang from the Hôtel de Crillon the number that Dimpsy had given her, she was unsurprised to find her call answered in French by a gruff male voice. In the light of Dimpsy's reputation on the St Wilhelmina's old girl grapevine, the surprise would have been if she hadn't got a man in residence.

Watched open-mouthed by her brother, Twinks dropped instantly into perfect, accent-free French and asked the man about Dimpsy's whereabouts. From the response it seemed her question had touched a raw nerve. The man at the other end of the line launched into a diatribe about the fickleness of the female gender and even Twinks, whose knowledge of the language was exhaustive, picked up a few new Gallic swear words.

Finally managing to stem the flow of vituperation, she elicited the information that Dimpsy was almost definitely to be found at the Bistrot Julien in Rue des Panniers on the Rive Gauche. 'And should you find her,' was the man's histrionic parting shot, 'tell her that if she ever comes back here, she will find—not the living Eugène Blocque, but the corpse of Eugène Blocque!' His words ended in a violent burst of coughing.

'I shall certainly pass on the message,' said Twinks politely.

6

Le Bistrot Julien

To reach the Bistrot Julien they took a cab. 'What's that fumacious stench?' asked Blotto as they entered its murky interior.

'It's garlic.'

'And what's that when it's got its jim-jams on?'

Twinks tried to explain, but her brother couldn't

be made to understand why anyone would allow anything that smelt like that near anything they were planning to eat. He had a lot to learn about France.

The cab driver dropped them in the pitch darkness of an unlit Rue des Panniers and immediately drove off, grumbling about the large tip Twinks had given him. Enquiries as to where they'd find the Bistrot Julien had been met by his full repertoire of hand gestures and facial tics, but unfortunately no directions.

As their eyes accommodated to the darkness, Blotto, fumbling around in a doorway, encountered the firm flesh of a scantily clad young woman who seemed very anxious for him to accompany her somewhere. But he couldn't understand what she was suggesting they should do together when they got there. (That wasn't due to the language barrier—he wouldn't have understood what she was suggesting they should do together when they got there if she'd been speaking English.) The young woman stormed off with a very French flounce of disgust.

'I can see about as much as a mole in a coal-hole,' Blotto complained.

'Don't don your worry-boots,' said Twinks. 'I've got something that'll sort us out.' She reached into her reticule and produced one of those new-fangled electric torches. Because it belonged to her, it was of course silver-plated.

Directing its beam into the dingy doorways of the Rue des Panniers, Twinks didn't take long to find a discoloured brass plaque on which 'Bistrot Julien' had been etched. The frontage looked little different from the other run-down buildings in the street. On the walls plaster bulged and cracked. Through the grimy windows meagre candlelight flickered. 'Come on, Blotters,' said Twinks, as she pushed against the sagging wooden door.

The interior seemed only marginally less dark than the pitch-blackness outside. It hadn't been just the filth on the windows that had diminished the candlelight. The glow they gave was extremely feeble and it was a moment or two before Blotto and Twinks could take in their surroundings.

The tables all stood in shady alcoves, but few of them seemed to be occupied. There wasn't the excited buzz of conversation that Twinks remembered from visits to other Parisian eating places. The Bistrot Julien had all the conviviality of a morgue after a tram crash.

But before that impression had time to settle, Twinks was cheered by a voice shrieking her name and a lithe body hurtling across the room to envelop her in its arms.

'Twinks, darling!'

'Dimpsy, darling!'

'It's positively shrimpy to see you, Twinks!'

'Shrimpy with a sloozy bodice, Dimpsy!'

'Shrimpy with a sloozy bodice and rah-rahs, Twinks!'

At the end of this exchange, the two girls burst into high-pitched giggles. Blotto felt a bit left out. He hadn't expected to understand anything French people said, but Dimpsy Wickett-Coote was English, for the love of strawberries! He thought he should be able to understand the odd word. But all he could extract from their conversation was his sister's name.

Even Blotto, however, couldn't help noticing that

the girl hugging Twinks was a splendid piece of womanflesh. She was tall and her black hair was cut into a short page-boy bob. Under long lashes lurked black eyes like concupiscent sloes. And even the shapelessness of the man's jacket and trousers she wore could not disguise the generosity of her contours.

As Twinks's giggles subsided, she remembered her brother. 'Now did you ever meet Blotto, Dimpsy?'

'No-oh.' The girl elongated the vowel almost to breaking point before asking, 'Where have you been hiding this haunch of venison? It's just like when we were at St Wilhelmina's. You always did manage to get the tastiest tips of asparagus, Twinks.'

'Dimpsy, Blotto is not an amorous swain, you clip-clop. He's my bro.'

'Is he?' More elongated vowels. Dimpsy Wickett-Coote was extremely interested in what she saw in front of her. With his thatch of blond hair and dazzling blue eyes, Blotto did look, as ever, impossibly handsome. Dimpsy moved towards him, almost physically licking her lips.

But her progress was interrupted by a torrent of French (incomprehensible to Blotto) and the interposition of a small man in filthy overalls and a beret between the girl and her prey. Undisturbed by the cataract of vituperation that spilled through them, from his lips dangled a grubby cigarette from which emanated the aroma of burning tyres.

The sputum of unfamiliar words directed at Blotto resolved itself into the repetition of one. The man spat up into his face what sounded like 'Sallow! Sallow! Sallow!'

40

Now, though he'd been the despair of his French teacher (and all his other teachers) at Eton, at that moment Blotto had what he thought of as a linguistic brainwave. Perhaps the frog-muncher's language wasn't so difficult after all . . . Perhaps the poor thimbles used English words and just added an 's' to the beginning of them!

So Blotto responded, 'And hello to you too.'

'You are English?' said the man, switching languages. 'That makes things even worse! That the faithless Dimpsy should choose a porridge-eater for a lover!'

'As it happens,' Blotto thought he ought to point out, 'I don't actually like porridge.'

'That is of no importance. You are still attempting to steal my woman, you . . . *salaud*!'

'Hello,' Blotto again responded.

The man coughed.

'I think,' said Twinks judiciously, 'that we are at cross purposes.' Then in fluent French she told the angry little man that Dimpsy and Blotto had never met before and that there was no emotional relationship between them. He was to some extent mollified by this, though suspicion still gleamed in his eye. And Dimpsy looked downright disappointed.

The four of them were soon seated round a battered table with a zinc top. The Frenchman ensured that Dimpsy was not allowed to sit next to Blotto. After his show of aggression, he now took over the duties of a host, though with very bad grace and a lot of elaborate working of his lower lip. He didn't ask the newcomers what they wanted to drink, but waved the empty bottle on the table to a slatternly waitress, who brought a replacement, along with two more grubby glasses.

Twinks and Dimpsy were immediately into a catch-up session on their last few years, an overlapping duologue interrupted by many shrieks and outbursts of hysterical laughter.

Blotto smiled at his host. Since the facial response he received looked more like a sneer than anything else, he decided he should perhaps lighten the mood with a little conversation. 'What is it we're drinking, me old pineapple?' he asked.

'It is *absinthe*.'

'Oh.' Unsurprisingly, he hadn't heard of it.

'The foolish *gouvernement* have tried to ban *absinthe—les salauds*!'

'Hello,' said Blotto, who thought he was now getting the hang of this French conversation business.

'But here in Bistrot Julien they always keep a secret store of *absinthe—pour moi. Absinthe* is the lifeblood of art!' Blotto took a cautious sip of the murky fluid, as the man went on, '*Absinthe* takes your breath away.'

When Blotto had once more achieved normal respiration, he was forced to admit that the man was right.

'The *gouvernement* has no understanding of the artistic temperament. The banning of *absinthe* is just another example of the *petit bourgeois* minds that control our lives. An artist like Tacquelle should not be constrained by the regulations of tiny minds.'

'And sorry, who is this Tacquelle boddo we're talking about?'

The Frenchman drew himself up in his chair to his full height. It wasn't very high. 'I am Tacquelle.

42

Gaston Tacquelle. Are you telling me you are another of the *paysans* who have not heard of my work?'

'Just remind me what your work is, me old thimble?'

'I am a *T'ianguliste*.'

'Ah, that would explain it. I'm a bit of an empty revolver when it comes to musicians.'

'I am not a *musicien*!' cried the deeply affronted Gaston Tacquelle. *'Je suis T'ianguliste!* *T'iangulisme* is the latest *vague* in the world of arts. We the *T'iangulistes* will sweep out the dusty corridors of *Impressionisme*! We will sweep away the memory of such crowd-pleasing hypocrites as Picasso! We will—' But the impassioned painter was then interrupted by a ferocious bout of coughing.

'Nasty tickle you've got there, me old greengage,' said Blotto. 'Need some cough drops. Presumably a boddo can buy cough drops in France?'

'It is not . . . a "tickle" . . . I am suffering from. It is—' Tacquelle managed to gasp this out before his words were swallowed in another tide of phlegm.

Dimpsy interrupted her shrieking reminiscences with Twinks to explain, with an awestruck note of admiration in her voice, 'Gaston is suffering from the *phtisie*.'

'Is he?' asked Blotto with an equally awestruck note of incomprehension in his voice.

'She means "consumption",' added Twinks helpfully.

'Ah, eating too much. Funny, he does look as though he stuffs the old tongue-trap with—'

'No,' Twinks explained patiently. 'Dimpsy is talking about tuberculosis.' Another bewildered

43

look from Blotto. 'TB. An infection of the lungs.'

'Ah, yes. Read your semaphore—on the same page now. That's the one where the poor old greengages keep spitting out blood?'

'You're bong on the nose there, Blotto.'

'Oh. Haven't noticed you spitting blood, Mr Tacquelle.'

'Often I do, often I do,' asserted the *Trianguliste*, aggrieved at having his illness downplayed. 'Every morning my pillow looks like the field of Magenta.'

'Red pillow you've got, is it, me old cucumber?'

'Magenta was a battlefield,' Twinks explained patiently.

'But it is true,' Gaston Tacquelle insisted. 'Every morning my pillow is like this battlefield, stained with my lifeblood.'

'Some mornings,' said Dimpsy Wickett-Coote.

Blotto was unaware of the newly aggrieved look that the painter focused on her for again diminishing his medical condition. He was too preoccupied by the shocking implication in Dimpsy's words—that she might actually see Gaston Tacquelle *in the mornings*. He'd heard rumours of that kind of thing happening between young men and women who weren't married, but he'd always dismissed the notion as fanciful, something dreamed up by novelists, poets and similar bad tomatoes. Toad-in-the-hole, he thought with a mental whistle of amazement, Twinks does have some *modern* friends.

Sensitive to the reproof she had received from Gaston Tacquelle, Dimpsy over-compensated by building up the serious state of his health. 'Both lungs are infected,' she proudly asserted. 'Gaston is on borrowed time. He could die any day. It's very romantic.'

'You poor old thimble,' said Blotto to the spluttering painter, with appropriate compassion. But not too much. A charmless Frenchman remained a charmless Frenchman; the fact that he was dying did not make a great deal of difference.

'Tragically,' Dimpsy went on, 'Gaston may actually die before he's completed his *chef d'oeuvre.*'

'Well, I'll be snickered . . .' murmured Blotto. 'I didn't know he was a cook as well.'

Dimpsy Wickett-Coote was about to reply to this, but a slight shake of the head from her schoolfriend stopped her. 'So,' asked Twinks, 'what is his *chef d'oeuvre?*'

'It is in the *Tringuliste* style . . .'

'Of course.'

'And it is a nude . . .'

'Of course.'

'And the subject of the work . . .' Dimpsy Wickett-Coote's face became wreathed in the dimples from which she had perhaps acquired her nickname, 'is little *moi.*'

'Larksissimo!'

'I've been sitting for months.'

'Oh, it's not that long,' said Blotto. 'I mean, I know the service is a bit slow, no sign of anyone bringing menus or that kind of rombooley, but—'

'Dimpsy means,' Twinks interceded, 'that she's been sitting as an artist's model for months.'

'Ah. On the right hymn sheet, Twinks me old cigar-cutter.' Blotto turned to Dimpsy. 'So where do you sit? On a chair?'

'I lie on a *chaise longue.*'

45

'Oh, very French.'

'I have been sitting for Gaston every morning for the past three months. Every day his cough gets worse. Every day he is closer to his death. Every day the likelihood of his finishing his *chef d'oeuvre* diminishes.'

'If there's such a time pressure,' said Blotto, his face suffusing with the rare pinkish glow that appeared when he had an idea, 'why don't you sit for him in the afternoons as well?'

'Because in the afternoons,' Dimpsy replied dramatically, 'I sit for Eugène Blocque.'

Hearing the name, Gaston Tacquelle spat out the single word, '*Salaud!*'

'Hello,' said Blotto, who had fully caught on now.

'But why do you do that, Dimpsy,' asked Twinks, 'if time is so short for Gaston?'

'Because,' her friend replied operatically, 'Eugène is also dying of the *phtisie*.'

'So you have two amorous swains trying to finish painting you before they topple off with the TB?'

'That's it, Twinks my shrimparoo!' Dimpsy Wickett-Coote glowed with the excitement of the moment. 'Isn't it the most romantic thing you've ever heard?'

'Well—'

'Because Eugène Blocque and Gaston Tacquelle are the premier artists of the *Trianguliste* Movement! And I am muse to both of them! In future the curves of my body—or rather the triangles of my body—will be known to art lovers all around the world. I, Dimpsy Wickett-Coote, will be hailed as one of the most beautiful women in history!'

'Do not be so sure!' Tacquelle's coughing fit had

subsided sufficiently for him to speak again. 'Perhaps the painting will never be finished.'

'Oh, stuff a pillow in it, Gaston! Of course you will live long enough to finish the painting, I know you will!' exhorted Dimpsy, rather in the way she spoke to her partners when playing tennis. 'I will be recorded for posterity as one of the most beautiful women in history.'

'You misunderstand me, *ma cocotte*. I did not mean that I would not finish the painting because I would die.'

'Then what did you mean?'

'I meant that, as an artist—as a *Trianguliste*—my muse has to be the most beautiful woman in the world!'

'Yes, I know that,' said Dimpsy. 'And you told me that I was the most beautiful woman in the world.'

' "Was"—that is the important word—"was". Dimpsy *mon petit choufleur*, when I described you as the most beautiful woman—*la plus belle du monde*, I was drawing my conclusion from insufficient data.'

'What in the name of Robinson Crusoe do you mean?'

'I mean that I thought you, Dimpsy, were the most beautiful woman in the world . . . until this evening . . . when I saw Twinks.'

Oh, broken biscuits, thought Blotto, not again. This kind of thing was always happening with his sister and experience had told him that it could end up in quite a major gluepot. Awful when you've got two best friends from school being set against each other by some thimble-jiggler of a man. They were both breathsappers, for the love of strawberries! Who cared whether one had just a fairy thimblesworth of beauty more than the other? But experience had also told Blotto that it was just that kind of tiny detail that women did care about.

Not Twinks, of course. His sister was always a Grade A foundation stone. She didn't let thoughts of beauty go to her head. She didn't worry about whether she was the biggest eye-wobbler in the room (but then of course she always *was* the biggest eye-wobbler in the room, so she didn't need to worry about it).

But the expression on the face of Dimpsy Wickett-Coote showed that she didn't take such considerations so lightly. Having first focused on Gaston Tacquelle a look of contempt that would have frozen the pipes in one of those new-fangled central heating systems, she turned her withering eye on what clearly 'used to be' her best friend.

'You Jezebel!' she cried, showing a depth of biblical reference that spoke rather well for the education supplied at St Wilhelmina's Convent.

Twinks shrugged her elegant shoulders. 'I'm not going to apologize, Dimpsy, because I haven't done anything.'

'No? You have deliberately set your cap at my man!'

'I can assure you that if I ever were to "set my cap" at any man—an eventuality that I regard as extremely unlikely—it would be at something with rather more "bottom" than this specimen.' At times Twinks could sound amazingly like her mother, the Dowager Duchess.

She looked down with pity at Gaston Tacquelle, who gazed up at her in adoration.

At that moment the outside door opened and

there irrupted into Bistrot Julien another small angry Frenchman in beret and paint-spattered overalls. To his lip too was fixed a tyre-burning cigarette. He pinioned Gaston Tacquelle with an eye that ripped into him like an auger. *'Salaud!'* he hissed.

'Hello,' said Blotto, really getting into the swing of things now.

Dimpsy Wickett-Coote stepped across to the newcomer and pressed her magnificent body against him. 'Eugène,' she purred. 'You may have all that you have ever desired! I will be completely yours!'

'You mean, *ma petite cochonette*,' the man asked, 'that you will sit for me in the mornings as well as the afternoons?'

'Of course I will! That way you will have a much better chance of finishing your *chef d'oeuvre*! And I will be immortalized in a painting by the greatest of the *Triangulistes*!'

'Eugène Blocque—"the greatest of the *Triangulistes*"?' Gaston Tacquelle spat out the words in a fusillade of spit and contempt. *'C'est affreux, c'est ridicule!* The only *Trianguliste* who will be venerated by posterity will be Gaston Tacquelle!'

Eugène Blocque gave one of those shrugs of contempt involving his whole face that only the French can do. (Blotto subsequently spent many hours trying to perfect it in front of his shaving mirror before concluding that Englishmen's lips weren't built the right way. Not that that worried him, of course. There were so many other benefits to being English.)

'I will be venerated,' cried Eugène Blocque,

49

'because I will have painted the definitive *Trianguliste* depiction of the most beautiful woman in the world! Dimpsy Wickett-Coote!'

He turned to face the object of his adoration, but in doing so he found Twinks in his eye line. '*Sacré bleu,*' he murmured. 'What a fool I have been—*quel idiot*! For so long I have believed that Dimpsy is the most beautiful—*la plus belle du monde*—but up until now I have been blind. Until this moment I had not seen you, *ma cherie*! What is your name?'

It was entirely possible that Twinks might have answered his question, had not Gaston Tacquelle, by now mad with jealousy, hurled himself at his rival, uttering what Blotto thought must be 'ghastly imprecations' (ghastly imprecations are recognizable in most languages).

Eugène Blocque came back with some ghastly imprecations of his own and within seconds the two painters were scrabbling on the floor, exchanging fisticuffs. Soon their shouted oaths gave way to coughing so violent that it seemed unlikely either of them would ever complete his *chef d'oeuvre*.

Suddenly the bistrot's front door again burst open to admit, muffled up in a tweed Ulster coat and scarf, the Marquis of Bluntleigh.

The moment he saw Twinks, he dropped down on one knee and declared, 'I have followed you all the way from England, Twinks. It is impossible for me to live without you. You are the most beautiful woman in the world!'

Twinks did not even acknowledge his presence. Taking an astonished Dimpsy Wickett-Coote by the hand, and saying, 'There are things we need to talk about, my girl,' she led her out into the

50

Parisian murk. The shabby door clattered shut behind them.

Buzzer Bluntleigh looked with puzzlement at the grappling *Triangulistes* on the floor, then turned a bemused eye on Blotto.

'Strange beasts, women, aren't they?' he said and received a nod of sympathy. 'I thought I'd got the plan to end all plans—chasing your sister all the way over to Paris and then telling her she was the most beautiful woman in the world. Wheeze had to be a copper-bottomed winner with the rest nowhere. And then the filly just walks out on me. I don't think I'm probably the first man to have aired the question, but *what do women want*? I mean, do you think there's anything else I could have done?' asked the Marquis in desperation.

'You could have tried coughing,' said Blotto.

7

La Rive Gauche

'Oh, it's all guff and toffee,' said Twinks impatiently. 'I didn't pongle over to Paris simply to be squabbled over by amorous swains. I'm here to find the stenchers who snaffled the Tawcester Towers' Gainsborough and Reynolds.'

She looked moodily out from the high windows in their suite at the Hotel de Crillon on to a frosty Place de la Concorde. French people, lagged in coats and scarves, hurried on their way to do whatever it was that French people did.

It was rarely that Blotto saw his sister in a bad

mood. Like his, the needle of her barometer was set permanently to 'Sunny'. But the events of that morning had been enough to put lumps in anyone's custard.

They had risen early, leaving the Hôtel de Crillon before breakfast. From past experience they both knew that nothing sharpened the appetite like a confrontation with a couple of malefactors.

They had taken a horse-drawn cab. (A number of these still existed in Paris, catering quaintly for the tourist trade.) And Twinks had given very specific instructions to the driver. First to La Rue des Folies-de-Grandeur in the Cinquième Arrondissement, and from there to La Place Biscuit de Garibaldi.

As they got out of the cab, excitement sparkled in the eyes of both siblings. This was the bit of every investigation that they really enjoyed— coming face to face with the perpetrators. Granted, in this particular case their journey had been fairly straightforward, but that didn't mean that the next few moments would be pure creamy éclair.

It didn't take long for their hopes to be dashed. The moment they approached the east side of Les Appartements Clichy, they saw that the doors and windows of their target had been boarded up.

The birds—the Vicomte and Vicomtesse de Sales-Malincourt or whoever they really were— had flown.

*   *   *

That was the reason why a testy silence had hung

between Blotto and Twinks as the cab clip-clopped back to the Hôtel de Crillon. And why Twinks was more irritated than she normally might have been by the excess of masculine attention that she had encountered in Le Bistrot Julien the previous evening.

Her brother tried to calm her, taking on the voice that he used when his hunter Mephistopheles had been disturbed by a pheasant breaking cover. 'Look, you ought to know the runner and riders by now, Twinks me old shoe-tree. Every time you waft into a room anywhere, some poor trumble's going to fall for you like a guardsman in a heatwave. You should be used to it. It's just part of the job of being Twinks. Surely the penny's gone in the slot for that one by now?'

'Well, it's a real stye in the eye.' His sister moved disconsolately to the window. 'And I don't like the threat it poses to my friendship with Dimpsy.'

'Why does it pose a threat, me old jar of mint sauce? All you have to do is ignore the amorous swains. Let them moon and mawk as much as they want to—just don't take any notice. And, come on, this Blocque and Tacquelle circus act are hardly our sort of boddos. No reason why you should ever see either of them again.'

'But I have to see them again.'

'Why?'

'Because they are my *entrée*.'

A furrow appeared in Blotto's patrician brow. 'You're going to eat them?'

'No, bro. Blocque and Tacquelle are my *entrée* to the Parisian art world.'

'Ah. Thinking of buying a painting, are you, Twinks?'

'No, but in the art world there will not only be painters, but also another kind of person . . . ?'

She let the implication dangle for him. 'People to clean their brushes?' suggested Blotto.

'Not them. I refer to art thieves.'

'Ah.'

'To find the art thieves in the art world, one must first infiltrate that art world.'

'And how do you propose doing that, Twinks me old library steps?'

'It is simple. I will take over Dimpsy's role as a model for Blocque and Tacquelle.'

Blotto was shocked. 'What, in the . . . um . . . ? Without any . . . ? You know, I mean, not wearing any . . . ? Because I'm not sure the old mater would—'

His sister overrode him. 'Usually an artist's model justifies taking her clothes off "in the cause of art". I will be doing it for an even greater purpose. I will be doing it "in the cause of investigation"!'

Blotto's sense of impropriety evaporated. 'Oh well, in that case, fair biddles to you.'

'I am having my first session this afternoon with Eugène Blocque. Dimpsy always did her afternoons with him.'

'Good ticket.'

'And then tomorrow morning I will be modelling for Gaston Tacquelle.'

'Hoopee-doopee, Twinks. So it will be your jolly old body that will be remembered by posterity as the crowning achievement of the *Trianguliste* Movement?'

A shrug of the slender shoulders dismissed the importance of such a thought. 'My only reason for

54

doing it, Blotters, is so that I can track down the two stolen Ruperts.'

'Yes, of course. On the same page with you about that. Erm . . . one thing?'

'What, Blotto?'

'Well, your taking over the modelling duties for Blocque and Tacquelle is all tickey-tockey, I'm sure, but isn't Dimpsy going to be absolutely fumacious about it? I mean, yesterday she was being told she was the most beautiful woman in the world, and suddenly you've got that billet and she's cast out among the also-rans and uglies. From what I've heard, women don't take kindly to a return to the ranks.'

'Dimpsy may be upset at the moment,' said his sister judiciously, 'but I have devised a way of chewing that particular rusk.'

'Beezer. I knew you would have.'

'It involves you, Blotto.'

'Good ticket, Twinks!' Her words cheered him. He'd been rather worried about being left out of the investigation. He couldn't envisage much of a role for himself sitting in Blocque and Tacquelle's draughty studios watching his sister being transformed into triangles. It would be embarrassing, apart from anything else . . . if Twinks hadn't got any . . . oh, biscuits, thought Blotto.

But what his sister said next wasn't quite such creamy éclair. 'Dimpsy will only feel put out if she does not have an amorous swain on hand. And, as you can't have helped twigging last night, she very much likes the look of you, Blotto . . .'

Oh, broken biscuits, he thought. 'But, Twinks me old coal-scuttle, I can't—'

Remonstrance, as he knew it would be, was vain. His sister had planned everything. And, for his sister's plan to work, he had at least to pretend romantic interest in Dimpsy Wickett-Coote. What a gluepot! She was a tasty enough joint of womanflesh, but all the same . . .

He had hardly found his feet after this first assault on his equilibrium, when he was hit by another. 'Then, Blotto, there is also the matter of the Marquis of Bluntleigh.'

'Old Buzzer?'

'Yes. His arrival in Paris is most inconvenient. Having him around, panting like a pop-eyed lapdog, is just the sort of thing to hobble my investigation.'

'*Our* investigation.'

'Yes, our investigation, of course, Blotto. We are in this together . . .'

'Hoopee-doopee!'

'. . . and you have a vital role to play in the next stage of that investigation.' He beamed his gratitude. 'Because what I want you to do, Blotto, is to head Buzzer off at the pass.'

'Sorry, not reading your semaphore?'

'I want you to keep the Marquis of Bluntleigh entertained.'

Visions of a repeat of his unwelcome duty at Tawcester Towers rose ominously in Blotto's mind.

They didn't get any less ominous when his sister continued, 'There are lashings of really good art galleries in Paris.'

Oh, biscuits shattered into a million tiny pieces, thought Blotto.

The studio of Eugène Blocque was up a series of rickety stairways on the top floor of a sagging building not far from Le Bistrot Julien. It was a gloomy attic, one side of which had been opened out and glassed in, presumably to let in the light. But the windows were so cracked and discoloured, so slime-stained and leaf-bestuck, that very little of the watery November sunshine could trickle through.

Within the studio everything was layered with sticky grime. The air was a foetid cocktail of sweat, cheap perfume, car-tyre cigarette smoke, mouse droppings and elderly Camembert. Every surface was so spattered with paint that it was a miracle that the painter had ever managed to get anything on the canvas.

And yet against the noxious walls were stacked piles of presumably finished paintings. From what Twinks could see of them as she entered the squalor, they were all more or less identical, assemblages of triangles in colours that ran through that small segment of the spectrum between mustard and gravy.

Seeing where her eyes were straying, Eugène volunteered that the canvases were all nude portraits of former models. 'And when I say former models, of course what I mean is former lovers.'

'Larksissimo!' said Twinks. 'But in my case, I should warn you not to count your blue tits before they're born.'

'*Je ne comprends pas*. What do you mean?'

'I mean you should not assume that I will ever become your lover. Because I won't.'

He looked bewildered by her words. 'But it is how things work here on *la Rive Gauche*. It is *la vie parisienne*. Artists always sleep with their models.'

'Not in my case.'

'All right. Maybe not on the first sitting, but—'

'Never!' cried Twinks. And in her azure eye was the steely look of Lyminsters past, practised in the business of facing down Frenchmen from Agincourt and before. The expression had its customary effect and Eugène Blocque was silent.

'So where's the painting you were working on with Dimpsy?'

'I have destroyed it.'

'But you had been doing it for months. All that hard work . . .'

'When I started the work, I thought I was painting the most beautiful woman in the world. Now I know that is not the case! Of what possible use is a half-finished painting of the second most beautiful woman in the world?' This impassioned outburst brought on a fierce paroxysm of coughing.

'Have you seen someone about that cough?' asked Twinks solicitously.

'What is the use of seeing someone? What does a *médecin* know? There is no cure for the *phtisie*.'

'But are you sure that what you've got is the *phtisie*?'

Blocque was affronted by the suggestion. 'Of course it is the *phtisie*. It is of the *phtisie* that I am dying,' he added proudly.

'But maybe you don't need to die. There are sanatoria in Switzerland which have brought about cures. And a warmer climate can help. I've been told that there are doctors in the South of France who—'

'*Tais-toi!* I will not hear of such ideas. *Le Triangulisme est un mouvement parisien.* I cannot work away from *la Rive Gauche.*'

'But if you took a bit of time off in the South of France you might build up your strength to . . .'

But Twinks's arguments had no effect. Eugène Blocque was determined to stay in Paris to complete his greatest work—what he kept referring to as *le chef d'oeuvre du Triangulisme*—even if he died in the attempt. In fact, he gave the impression that he'd be jolly disappointed if he didn't die in the attempt.

Twinks had no worries of the prudish kind. Used from an early age to being dressed and undressed by servants, she was unconcerned by her own nakedness. And though she had never before spent an entire afternoon naked on a grubby *chaise longue* in the sole company of a lubricious Frenchman, she remained totally unfazed by the experience. Without actually spelling it out, Twinks had somehow communicated to Eugène Blocque that he had only to lay one finger on her and he'd soon be smashing out through his own grubby window to land way down on the cobbles below.

So, while the artist brushed away at his canvas, converting her perfect contours into beige triangles, Twinks interrogated him about the criminal side of the Parisian art world.

*   *   *

The following morning, in another equally squalid studio, also on *la Rive Gauche*, she went through a more-or-less verbatim repetition of the same scene with Gaston Tacquelle. He too had destroyed his work-in-progress on Dimpsy Wickett-Coote. He too refused to seek medical help to cure his *phtisie*. He too was deeply affronted at the idea of a model not sleeping with the artist who was painting her. And he too recognized the wisdom of not laying a finger on Twinks.

But neither of the *Triangulistes* could give her any pointers that might help her to track down the so-called Vicomte and Vicomtesse de Sales-Malincourt.

8

Les Deux Mangetouts

'And is it not inevitable that, if one subscribes to Schopenhauer's view of the *Wille zum Leben*, one must inevitably have a *Weltanschauung* that is *pessimiste*?'

'Erm, possibly,' said Blotto.

'But at the same time Schopenhauer recognizes the *imperative* of the sexual urge, though he believes that in the pursuit of *l'amour*, *l'homme moyen sensuel* is doomed to disappointment. For it is in the nature of all human ambitions to aspire to an ideal which can never, *ipso facto*, be *réalisable*, *n'est-ce pas*?'

'You could be right,' said Blotto.

He wasn't feeling at his most comfortable. Given that his most comfortable was astride Mephistopheles galloping over the beloved acres of Tawcester Towers, this was no great surprise. The café Les Deux Mangetouts, was about as far from that ideal as was possible. They had come there on the recommendation of Dimpsy Wickett-Coote, who was an *habituée* of this large, busy venue in Saint-Germain-des-Prés.

She was there with him, presenting Blotto with the ongoing challenge of obeying his sister's instructions to make Dimpsy believe he held a candle for her, while his every instinct told him that the only thing he wanted to do was to blow that candle out.

Then there was another stye in the eye in the form of the Marquis of Bluntleigh. Deprived of the presence of Twinks—and indeed having had his declaration of love ignored by her—Buzzer was in low spirits. He spoke distractedly of 'doing something stupid' . . . even of trying to win his beloved's heart by writing her a poem in French.

And to compound Blotto's irritation, the waiter—like all waiters in Les Deux Mangetouts—insisted on delivering a lecture on philosophy rather than taking his order. It was as bad as rain stopping play when only two runs were needed for the victory.

'But then of course when Nietzsche developed Schopenhauer's *Wille zum Leben* into his own *Wille zur Macht*, we find ourselves challenged by the syllogistic proposition that—'

'Look, would you please just get us three coffees!' bellowed Blotto (people of his class had never had any inhibitions about talking loudly in cafés—or anywhere else, come to that).

The waiter did not appear to be put down by being shouted at. He took it philosophically (as

61

indeed he took everything else), and went off to get their order.

There was a silence. Blotto did not let his eye linger long on the Marquis—that hangdog expression was far too dispiriting. Dimpsy Wickett-Coote was a far more attractive sight. Quite a breathsapper, in fact. He could imagine lots of boddos falling for her like gallowsmen on a trapdoor. He'd have been tempted himself, but for the complications that always come with women. The danger of somehow finding you've ended up getting married to one . . . and then having your hunting rights curtailed.

But he had promised Twinks . . . And it was in the cause of their investigation. His sister had specifically asked him to make doe eyes at Dimpsy. He had to think of something. A compliment. Yes, that'd be beezer. He'd heard from many sources that women really liked compliments.

Blotto brought his brain to bear on the subject for a long moment. Then, directing the full beam of his bonhomie on Dimpsy Wickett-Coote, he said, 'You're as beautiful a sight to a man's eyes as a fox being torn apart by hounds.'

The expression which greeted this remark suggested that the image didn't rank as high in Dimpsy's pantheon of perfection as it did in his. 'Stuff a pillow in it, Blotto,' she said.

Clearly he wasn't living up to Twinks's hopes for him. He cleared his throat and tried again.

'What I mean to say, Dimpsy, is that you're as beautiful as a well-linseed-oiled cricket bat.'

This second attempt also got a look that would have iced over the contents of an erupting volcano. What on earth did the woman want, for the love of strawberries? He had another pop at the partridge.

'What I'm really trying to say, Dimpsy, is that you're as beautiful as . . .'

While Blotto fumbled through his meagre stock of similes, he was surprised to hear his sentence completed by another voice. '. . . as a dragonfly alighting on a lily leaf in Monet's garden.'

The accent was American and it belonged to a burly man with black hair and moustache who was approaching their table. He wore a shapeless three-piece tweed suit over a khaki shirt and dark green tie. In his wake came a slighter figure, a clean-shaven man whose dark hair was parted in the centre.

Clearly the newcomers were known to Dimpsy Wickett-Coote. Leaping to her feet, she threw her long arms around both of them. 'Chuck! Scott! How shrimpalicious to see you!' Her voice was nearly as high-pitched as when she had greeted Twinks the night before. She turned to make the introductions. 'Blotto, Buzzer, these two reprobates are terrific chums of mine—Chuck Waggen and Scott Frea!'

Forgoing the courtesy of handshakes, the two Americans brought chairs up to the table and quickly summoned the waiter. After a brief discussion of the influence of Platonic Dialogue on Kant's Transcendental Aesthetic, they ordered a bottle of whisky, asked the waiter to bring the soda syphon, and began to drink with single-minded dedication.

'Blotto? What kind of a name's that?' demanded the larger man, the one called Chuck Waggen.

'It's a nickname.'

'Holy cats, I never figured you were christened

63

with it. And what do you do, Blotto?'

'Do?' It was an unexpected and difficult question. 'Well, I, er . . . um . . .' Then he had the brilliant idea of turning the tables on the American by asking, 'Why, what do you do?'

'I write. So does Scott.'

'Ah.'

'Do you?'

'Yes, I can write,' asserted Blotto.

'What do you write *on*?'

'Um . . . chequebooks . . . tailors' bills . . . that kind of thing.' Seeing the puzzlement in the thickset man's eyes, Blotto thought he'd try another reversal. 'Why, what do you write on?'

'Life. Death. Death in the morning. And at other times of day. Drink. Boxing. Bulls. Stuff.'

'Hoopee-doopee,' said Blotto.

'So what do you do?' Chuck Waggen asked again.

The question couldn't be ducked a second time, so Blotto replied airily, 'Oh, this and that.' Cannily he realized this was not the moment to mention criminal investigation. 'Play a bit of cricket . . .' he went on. 'Hunting . . .'

The muscular man's eyes lit up. 'I like hunting. Hunting is good. Not so good perhaps as being with a dame. But it's good. What kind of gun do you use, Blotto?'

'Ah. I don't use a gun.'

'What, you wrestle the beasts down with your bare hands? Like with the bulls in Pamplona?'

'No, I hunt . . . we hunt . . . I mean one hunts in England with hounds.'

'Ah. Yes. I heard of that some place. Kinda takes away the fun, doesn't it?'

'Well, no, it—' But before he could articulate his

impassioned defence of the hunting he knew and loved, Blotto was interrupted by the other American, Scott Frea.

'Are you not a drinking man?' he asked Blotto.

'Oh, yes, I drink. And eat too,' he added helpfully.

'No, I mean proper drinking. Is that coffee in your cup?'

'Yes.'

'Then why don't you drink a man's drink?'

'You mean alcohol? Well, it's a bit early in the day for me to—'

'Tommyrot! There's no time of the day too early for alcohol. Isn't that right, Chuck?'

'Sure. First thing I do in the morning is have a drink. That is, after I've had an hour's swim in the Seine, boxed ten rounds and written two thousand words. Then I have a drink. Can you hold liquor, Blotto?'

'Well, I can if it's in a glass. Not in my bare hands, though. And, Scott, do you do the same as Chuck? Get some writing done before you start drinking?'

'No, I get some drinking done before I start writing.'

'And then you often don't get round to doing the writing,' said Chuck Waggen on a bellow of laughter. He turned his dark eyes on Blotto. 'I could drink you under the table. Because I'm a man. Are you a man, Blotto?'

'Oh yes.' The questions were getting easier.

Chuck Waggen turned a contemptuous look on his friend. 'And what about you, Scott? Are you a man?'

'Sure.'

This was rewarded by another bellow of laughter. 'You'll never be half the man that I am.'

'You're right, Chuck,' Scott Frea conceded.

'Nobody will ever be half the man that I am.'

Blotto was a little disturbed by this kind of talk. Being brought up properly—in other words, as an English gentleman—he knew that one of the worst social solecisms that could be committed was 'showing off'. This had been dinned into him from his earliest youth by the Dowager Duchess, by an ever-more-despotic sequence of nannies and by his education at Eton. Whatever manly feats one had achieved, it was really bad form to crow about them. And the correct way to respond to a compliment was with an embarrassed shake of the head and the sheepish words, 'Don't talk such spoffing guff.'

Certainly the last thing one should do was to talk in the way Chuck Waggen was talking. But then he was American, Blotto concluded generously, so he probably didn't know any better.

While he was thinking this, the catalogue of Waggen's self-defined superiority continued. Not only could he outdrink anyone, he could also outwrite anyone, outhunt anyone, outfish anyone, outfight anyone. And when it came to the ladies . . .

Blotto's upbringing had also taught him that it was unbelievably bad form for a man to talk about his amorous conquests. It was something he would never do—even though, in his case, his amorous conquests were always accidental. Blotto's allergic reaction to the idea of matrimony meant that he would never make a first move on a girl. But in spite of that, women did have a habit of falling for him like giraffes on an ice rink.

It was a phenomenon he could never really understand. Not only had his upbringing taught him to play down his achievements, it had also given him a suitably low estimate of his worth. That was the aim of a British upper-class education, after all—to produce young men who could organize foreign people in the Empire, but who never succumbed to introspection or personal vanity.

To Blotto the idea that an impossibly handsome and honourable second son of a duke might be an attractive target for a young woman to get in her sights had never occurred.

Continuing his theme of amorous conquests, Chuck Waggen now turned the full beam of his personality on to Dimpsy Wickett-Coote. After the glow he had given her with his dragonfly compliment, she had become rather bored with the subsequent direction of the conversation. She felt excluded, sitting in silence beside the lugubrious Marquis of Bluntleigh. Dimpsy needed masculine attention and adoration the same way that a sunflower needs the sun.

She certainly blossomed when Chuck Waggen told her, 'You're the most beautiful woman in the world.'

Part of Blotto felt jealous that he hadn't come up with such a simple compliment, rather than pongling around with comparisons to dismembered foxes and cricket bats. But another part felt hugely relieved. If Chuck Waggen was going to make up to Dimpsy Wickett-Coote, then that rather let him off the hook. Twinks had wanted her friend to have an amorous swain and had nominated her brother for the role. But surely this muscle-bound American writer would do the business just as well?

And if Chuck was pressing his suit with Dimpsy and the Marquis of Bluntleigh was still wallowing in his own gloom, Blotto had the perfect opportunity to continue his investigation into the disappearing Ruperts. Twinks had often told him that clues could come from the most unlikely sources, and that a good way of eliciting information was to get people drunk.

Well, Scott Frea was an extremely unlikely source, and he was managing to get himself drunk quite satisfactorily. So Blotto turned to him and asked, 'I say, Scott me old pineapple, do you know anything about Art Theft?'

'Art Theft? Hell, I don't know. There are just so many jazz musicians around in Paris these days.'

'No, not Art Theft the person . . . if indeed there is a boddo of that name. I'm talking about the theft of art. I just wondered if—'

But Blotto had chosen the wrong moment to pursue his investigation. Scott Frea's ongoing rivalry with his compatriot meant that he couldn't allow Chuck Waggen free rein in pressing his suit with Dimpsy. Scott had also to enter the lists. He didn't go for the fancy stuff, either. He just said, 'Dimpsy, you really are the most beautiful woman in the world.'

His words certainly had the right effect on her. Having both Americans praising her beauty made Dimpsy Wickett-Coote swell up like one of those Japanese paper flowers that Blotto remembered from his nursery. A beam of contentment settled on her features as the two rivals vied to outcompliment each other. The beam of contentment on Blotto's face, prompted by the fact that there were now two other men paying court to Dimpsy, was almost as wide.

'I want to take you on my next big-game hunting trip to Africa,' offered Chuck Waggen to his latest object of adoration.

'I want to take you to dance with me in the hottest jazz club in Paris,' counterbid Scott Frea.

'I will immortalize you in a book as a woman. One who suffers the privations of war. And still remains sexy.'

'I will immortalize you in a book in which you are beautiful, enigmatic and slightly unhinged.'

'You will find in me. A lover. With the strength of a bull.'

'You will find in me a lover who is very sensitive and irresistibly neurotic.'

'I will fight any man who so much as looks at you.'

'I will not fight, but I have my own ways of—'

Whether the situation would have developed into open fisticuffs and—given the disparity in physique between the two Americans—the inevitable flooring of Scott Frea was a question destined never to be answered. Because at that moment the interior of Les Deux Mangetouts was irradiated by the entrance of Twinks. A silence descended on the café. Even the waiter stopped in the middle of his explanation of Spinoza's early espousal of Descartian Dualism to a man who only wanted to order a quick brandy.

The two writers, in the grip of a power stronger than themselves, turned instantly towards the new arrival. As they did so, the glow on the face of

Dimpsy Wickett-Coote vanished as quickly as a manifesto promise after an election.

'Holy smoke!' said Chuck Waggen. 'I've just seen the most beautiful woman in the world.'

'I've just seen the most beautiful woman in the world,' said Scott Frea. 'And what's more, Chuck, I saw her first!'

The two writers squared up to each other, ready to do battle for the love of Twinks.

It would be hard to say whether Dimpsy Wickett-Coote's or the Marquis of Bluntleigh's face looked as if it had swallowed the larger lemon.

But when Dimpsy refocused her doe eyes on him, Blotto looked as if he'd swallowed the largest lemon in the known universe.

9

Art for Heaven's Sake!

Blotto felt as though he was reliving one of the most boring times of his life. He'd found giving the Marquis of Bluntleigh the tour of the Tawcester Towers art collection bad enough, but at least there had been a finite number of Ruperts to be pointed out (and, as it turned out, two fewer than there should have been). But the Louvre . . . The Louvre went on for ever. It seemed to have no beginning and no end . . . just room after room after room . . . And all of them full of spoffing paintings!

Now Blotto knew he had limitations when it came to the knowledge of art—he had limitations when it came to the knowledge of anything—but there were paintings he liked. A hunting scene, a picture of a ship or a horse, even a naval battle . . . he could respond to those. They made him think of things he enjoyed. But there were distressingly few hunting scenes, pictures of ships, horses or naval battles in the Louvre. Just, so far as he could see, endless scenes from the Bible. And although Blotto had nothing against the Bible, he knew very little about it (he was Church of England, after all). And the few bits he did know (vestigial memories from scripture lessons at Eton) didn't interest him at all.

It wasn't just what hung on the walls that depressed him about the Louvre, it was also what was standing on the floors. Now Blotto was not a snob; he just had an attitude to the oikish classes that had been handed down through generations of the Lyminster family. But, unlike many people of his breeding, he recognized that the feudal system had come to an end. He had no argument with the idea that estate workers at Tawcester Towers should be paid (though not very much). And he had a common touch. He thought nothing of spending hours round the garages with Corky Froggett, discussing the latest in automobiles. And at Christmas he was happy to entertain the servants to magnanimous pats on the back and half-glasses of sherry. No, he thought the oikish classes were all very fine in their place.

So long as they kept in that place. So long as they didn't start lording it round ancestral buildings like the Louvre, acting as if their presence in such environments was a right rather than a privilege.

Blotto couldn't help but find their behaviour

irksome. There were too many of them, for a start. And then, to compound his discomfort, most of them were speaking foreign languages. So far as Blotto was concerned, that rather put the lid on the jam jar. For the love of strawberries, a public building like the Louvre ought to maintain the most basic of admission strictures, and only allow in people who spoke English!

Not only was Blotto cast down by the unknown throng that surrounded him, he was further vinegared off by his closer companions. Being upstaged by Twinks in the affections of Chuck Waggen and Scott Frea had not improved the mood of Dimpsy Wickett-Coote. She wore the pout of a star player who'd been left out of the school lacrosse team. Nor did the Marquis of Bluntleigh look any more chipper. He wasn't responding well to being totally ignored by the object of his adoration and bundled off on a tour of the Louvre with her utterly uninformed brother.

'How can I persuade Twinks I'm the right boddo for her?' he kept asking mournfully. 'Come on, Dimpsy, you're a woman. What would be the way into your heart?'

'Well, telling me I am the most beautiful woman in the world used to be a good ticket,' she replied, not without bitterness, 'but then hearing the same person say the same thing to someone else minutes later tends to take the icing off that particular Swiss bun.'

'Ah,' sighed the Marquis of Bluntleigh glumly. 'I've tried that approach with Twinks, but she doesn't seem to notice me. What about art? Do women respond to art—you know, to being someone's muse?'

Blotto remembered what Twinks had told him and so didn't go wading in with talk of stable blocks. He just waited for Dimpsy's response.

'Well, it could be the right size of pyjamas,' she said disconsolately. 'The idea of inspiring great art does appeal to a woman's vanity. Like being the model for the greatest work of the *Trianguliste* Movement—that'd tick the clock all right.' She sighed with acid wistfulness. 'Until, of course, you find out that the canvas of you has been destroyed because the artist has met someone else he finds more beautiful than you are. That tends rather to pancake a girl's aspirations.'

This prompted another glum nod from Buzzer Bluntleigh. 'And what about poetry? Aren't women supposed to respond to boddos writing poems about them?'

'Yes, that would be quite shrimpy.' Dimpsy Wickett-Coote was reflective for a moment. 'I've never actually had someone write a poem about me.' Then the old rivalry reasserted itself. 'Has Twinks had poems written about her?'

'I wrote her one,' the Marquis of Bluntleigh replied with an expression of deep apology.

'And what effect did it have on her?'

'I've no idea. She hasn't mentioned it.'

'Ah.' The potential jealousy in Dimpsy's expression receded.

The Marquis turned to their host. 'I say, Blotto. Twinks did get that poem I wrote for her, didn't she?'

'Could hardly fail to, could she, Buzzer me old charabanc? You thrust it personally into her dainty little mitt.'

'Yes, but did she read it?'

'Oh yes.'

'And what did she think of it?'

'Ah.' Blotto knew his reply had to be cautious. Didn't want to send the Marquis even deeper down into his current gluepot. To report that his sister had described his poem as 'total toffee' might be hurtful to the poor thimble, so all he said was, 'Tickey-tockey, Buzzer.'

'Is that what she thought of it?'

'No, it's just what I said.'

'Oh.' The expression on the Marquis of Bluntleigh's face suggested that Blotto hadn't been much help. Buzzer turned his attention back to Dimpsy Wickett-Coote. 'Do you think,' he asked, 'that a woman would be more impressed by a poem written in English or one written in French?'

'Well, I suppose it would depend on the nationality of the amorous swain who was writing the thing.'

'Yes. If it were someone English?'

'I suppose that might impress some women.'

'I think it would impress Twinks.'

'You might be right,' said Dimpsy. 'Twinks is such a Grade A brainbox she might be impressed by someone with a mastery of languages. Do you have a mastery of languages, Buzzer?'

'No.'

'A mastery of one language would do. So long as that language is French.'

'I speak as much French as I do Hottentot.'

'And how's your Hottentot?'

'Non-existent,' the Marquis of Bluntleigh confessed.

'But just a minute,' said Dimpsy. 'I'm sure someone told me that your mother was French.'

'Yes, she is.'

'Then surely you must speak the spoffing lingo.'

'No. My father was rather ashamed of the fact that he'd married someone French.'

'Well, you can see his point.'

'So he tried to pretend the mater was actually English.'

'Oh?'

'And he forbade her from speaking a word of French round the house. So I never heard any from her—not of course that I saw much of her, anyway.'

Dimpsy Wickett-Coote and Blotto nodded. That was perfectly reasonable. Mothers of their class kept away from their children as much as possible, allowing the business of upbringing to be delegated to a series of nursemaids and governesses. Until the age of sixteen, Dimpsy wouldn't have recognized her mother if she'd bumped into her on the street.

'I was thinking, Dimpsy . . .' the Marquis went on. 'You speak French, don't you?'

'Like a Breton onion seller, yes.'

'Well, maybe you could teach me enough French to write a poem for Twinks?'

'And what biddles would there be in that for me?' she asked cautiously.

'Well, if Twinks liked my poem and married me, then she'd be off the scene and Blocque and Tacquelle would have to go back to making do with you as the most beautiful girl in the world.'

The 'making do' was perhaps not the most tactful expression that he could have used, but, that blemish aside, Dimpsy Wickett-Coote was rather attracted to his proposal. 'I think it's a really sloozy idea, Buzzer. Let's find a café and get to work over something warm and alcoholic.'

'But I'm meant to be showing you round the Louvre,' Blotto objected. He was following Twinks's instructions and didn't want to let her down.

'I'm sure you can entertain yourself in here,' said Dimpsy tartly. 'Give the glad eye to the odd painting. Might provide a bit of a jockey-up to your knowledge of the visual arts, eh, Blotto? Because you're standing at this moment in front of the one picture in the world that even you are bound to recognize.'

Giving up on hopes of keeping his two guests with him, he turned to look at the painting Dimpsy had referred to. He saw a long-haired woman sitting with her hands folded against an indistinct background. On her yellowish face there was a vague expression. The expression on Blotto's face as he looked at her was equally vague.

'It is smaller than you expect perhaps?' asked a heavily accented male voice behind him.

He looked round to see that Dimpsy and the Marquis had gone, but in their place stood a couple in the robes of a Maharajah and his Rani.

'What's smaller than I expect?' asked Blotto.

'The *Mona Lisa*,' the man replied. 'The masterpiece perhaps of Leonardo da Vinci.'

'Ah,' said Blotto. He looked again at the painting. 'You could be right.'

'You are interested in art, I think?'

'Er . . . well . . . um . . .'

'My Rani and I are very interested in art. All the way from Pranjipur we come to see the famous artworks of Paris. How far have you come may I

76

ask, young man?'

'I've come from Tawcester Towers.'

Blotto always spoke the name of his home with the confidence that everyone in the world would have heard of it, but he still felt slight surprise when the pair nodded and the man said, 'We of course know this famous estate as the ancestral home of the Lyminster family.'

'You're bong on the nose there, me old pineapple.'

'Everyone in India has heard of the exploits of the Lyminster family. Particularly on the cricket field. You have not by any chance during your sojourn at Tawcester Towers been so fortunate as to encounter the Honourable Devereux Lyminster —the young man who once scored an unbeaten hundred and seventy-six in the Eton and Harrow match?'

Blotto smiled boyishly. 'I know the boddo you mean, yes.'

'If you could ever arrange an introduction for me to that gentleman,' said the Maharajah, 'I would be eternally in your debt.'

'So should I. I have for so long wished to meet him,' agreed the Maharajah's breathsapper of a wife.

'You want me to arrange a meeting for you with the Honourable Devereux Lyminster?' asked Blotto with a grin. 'Well, you know, I don't think that should be too hard a rusk to chew.'

*   *   *

He had just finished describing the cover drive that had brought up his hundred and was enjoying the

Indian couple's rapt admiration for his blow-by-blow account of the famous innings, when a thought struck Blotto. 'Bit of a long chance, us just meeting up in the Louvre like that, wasn't it?'

'Not strange at all, really,' said the man who had by now identified himself as the Maharajah of Pranjipur. 'In real life there occurs a level of coincidence that would not be tolerated in a work of fiction.'

They were sitting in a café in the Jardin des Tuileries. Blotto felt relieved to be away from all that art. And he was in a considerably mellower mood. Apart from actually playing the game, there was nothing he liked more than the retelling of his exploits on the cricket pitch. And he couldn't have asked for a more enthusiastic and attentive audience than the Maharajah and Rani of Pranjipur. Blotto found himself rather warming to the couple. Of course, they were foreign and there was nothing that could be done for them in that respect, poor thimbles, but at least they came from India, a country that was part of the British Empire. And, more importantly, a country that appreciated cricket.

Indeed the Maharajah seemed, from odd hints he dropped in the course of Blotto's narrative, to have played the game himself to quite a respectable level. He mentioned the names of great English players with appropriate reverence and appeared to understand every nuance of Blotto's description of how he readjusted the grip on his bat to deal with the notorious 'googly'.

Knowing the man was a cricketer put the Englishman at his ease. Nobody who understood the laws of the game could be a complete stencher.

78

As he looked into the earnest dark-brown face, Blotto found himself wondering whether the scar on the Maharajah of Pranjipur's cheekbone could have been caused by an errant cricket ball from a fast bowler.

He was impressed by the Rani too. One of the odd things Blotto had found in his dealings with women (who were, he knew, strange cattle in many ways) was how few of them had an understanding of—or even a liking for—cricket. But the Rani of Pranjipur definitely ticked the clock on that score. She listened intently to his reliving of the famous innings, seeming to regard every word that came out of his mouth as a rich jewel.

For a moment Blotto had the uncharacteristic thought that even matrimony might be tolerable if the female party to the contract appreciated cricket. Obviously he wasn't thinking straight, but he did find he was falling under the allure of the Rani of Pranjipur. She was foreign, of course, but a bit of a breathsapper . . . in a foreign sort of way.

Beautifully proportioned, and with a beautiful oval face. Perfect complexion . . . well, except for a small mole on her chin. But the blemish perversely seemed to increase rather than diminish her attractions.

Blotto had difficulty taking his eyes off her as he relived the crowning moment of his innings, the standing ovation he received from team-mates and opponents as he entered the Lord's pavilion after saving the honour of Eton. He related how embarrassed he had felt by all the attention and repeated the words with which he had responded to the compliments around him: 'Don't talk such toffee, you muffin-toasters. I'm not the pony who deserves a rosette. It was a spoffing team effort.'

A reverent silence followed the end of his narration. Then both the Maharajah and his Rani breathed sighs of admiration before he observed, 'It was very fortunate that we met beside the *Mona Lisa* this morning.'

'Mona who?'

'The painting.'

'Oh, the grumpy-faced yellow old fruitbat?'

'Exactly. Held by some people to be the most beautiful woman in the world.'

'Well, then those people need an urgent visit to the spec-doctor. Why, I can see a more beautiful woman at . . .' Blotto was within a mosquito's pimple of completing the sentence 'this table', when it occurred to him that some husbands got a bit funny about having their wives complimented. So he finished rather feebly 'almost any event I go to.'

'Her beauty may be a matter for discussion,' said the Maharajah of Pranjipur, 'but there is no doubt about her value.'

'Oh?'

'We are speaking of one of the most valuable paintings in the entire world. The *Mona Lisa* is worth hundreds of thousands of English pounds, possibly millions.'

Not for the first time, Blotto concluded that he never would understand the art world. If he had millions of English pounds, buying a picture of a grumpy yellow-faced woman would be so far down his list of potential purchases as to be invisible.

But the Maharajah of Pranjipur's words also prompted another reaction in his slow brain. A discussion about the value of paintings offered him the perfect cue to divert the conversation towards the subject of the investigation which he and Twinks were currently pursuing.

'So this *Mona Lisa* would be quite a target for art thieves, would it?' he demanded, with what he thought of as remarkable subtlety.

'Of course,' the Maharajah agreed. 'Indeed it has already been stolen once.'

'Toad-in-the-hole!'

'As a political gesture by an Italian nationalist.'

That sentence contained too many concepts that Blotto couldn't begin to understand, so he confined his reaction to an 'Oh.'

'But who will be so bold as to say,' the Maharajah continued, 'that the *Mona Lisa* will never be stolen again?'

At this he and his wife exchanged looks and giggles that could only be described as mischievous.

Not noticing this, Blotto continued his line of investigation. 'So the *Mona Lisa* would be worth more than a Gainsborough or a Reynolds?'

'Very considerably more.'

'Do you know anything about art thieves?' asked Blotto boldly.

The Indian couple exchanged another look. 'Maybe a little,' the Maharajah conceded.

'Because I'm in Paris with my sister Twinks trying to track down a couple of paintings that some spoffing lumps of toadspawn snaffled from our ancestral pile, Tawcester Towers.'

'Really?' The two spoke together, both Maharajah and Rani apparently surprised by this revelation.

'And we think—well, my sister worked out—'

81

Blotto was always punctilious about giving credit where credit was due—'that the Gainsborough and the Reynolds were snaffled by a couple of stenchers called the Vicomte and Vicomtesse de Sales-Malincourt.'

'And it is to confront them that you are here in Paris?' suggested the Maharajah.

'You've won the coconut! That's exactly what we're doing here.'

'Have you yet seen the malefactors you are seeking?'

'No. They'd moved out of the address we had for them.'

'Do you know what they look like?'

'Well, we know what they look like as the Vicomte and Vicomtesse de Sales-Malincourt, but you see, the thing is, these two stenchers are masters of disguise. So they could be dressed up as members of the Russian Royal Family . . . or Pearly Kings and Queens.'

'Or a maharajah and his wife?' suggested the Rani of Pranjipur.

They all had a good laugh at that preposterous idea, but then the Maharajah got serious. 'If you are genuinely trying to track down your Gainsborough and Reynolds, I have a suggestion for you. It is possible that we may be able to introduce you to some people who will know the whereabouts of the missing paintings.'

'Hoopee-doopee! That'd absolutely be the lark's larynx!' cried Blotto, once again lured by the prospect of making faster headway on their investigation than his sister.

'But these people,' the Maharajah went on, 'might expect payment for handing the goods

82

over.'

'That's outside the rule book!' complained Blotto. 'If these bad tomatoes stole the paintings, they don't deserve to get paid for returning them!'

'Are you sure about that?' The Maharajah smiled. 'Is it not a strong tradition among the aristocratic families of England, capturing members of rival dynasties and holding them to ransom?' Blotto was forced to admit that such behaviour was not unknown in the annals of Tawcester Towers. 'You would have to think of the money you paid as a ransom for the release of the two Ruperts.'

'Well, I'm not sure that . . .' But suddenly his words stopped. Blotto had a blinding moment of intuition, of the kind that came so very rarely to him and so frequently to his sister. 'How do you know that the Gainsborough and Reynolds I mentioned were both paintings of Ruperts?'

The Maharajah of Pranjipur looked nonplussed. Blotto pressed home his advantage, incisive as a prosecuting barrister in a murder trial. 'I didn't mention their names, did I?'

There was a silence, then the Rani said, 'Yes, I think you did, actually.'

'Oh.' Blotto's moment of potential glory had passed. He would have sworn he hadn't mentioned the word 'Rupert', but if the Maharajah's wife said he had . . . well, it wasn't done to question the word of a lady, was it?

'Anyway,' said the Maharajah of Pranjipur, once again businesslike, 'we will leave a message for you at the Hôtel de Crillon, with details of a rendezvous where you can meet the two people who are prepared to negotiate the return of your paintings. Whether you decide to make that meeting is up to you.'

'Just a minute,' said Blotto, in another moment of inspiration, 'I don't think I mentioned that I was staying at the Hôtel de Crillon.'

'I think you did, actually, yes,' said the Rani.

Once again, of course, he couldn't question the word of a lady.

'Anyway, my wife and I must be on our way.' The two Indians rose from the table.

'Hold back the hounds a moment!' cried Blotto, as a new idea came to him.

The Maharajah and his wife froze, while the Englishman looked searchingly into their faces. The words of Twinks came back to him, the details she had pointed out in the photographs sent by Professor Erasmus Holofernes. A mole and a scar!

Blotto concentrated furiously as he dredged the details up from his memory. A mole on the right-hand side of the chin and a scar high up on the left cheekbone. Was he within an ace of revealing that the Maharajah of Pranjipur and the Rani of Pranjipur were in fact the Vicomte and Vicomtesse de Sales-Malincourt *in disguise*? Was he about to unmask the running sores who'd stolen the two Ruperts from Tawcester Towers?

But when he looked closely at the pair, his hopes evaporated. The mole was on the left-hand side of the Rani's chin. And the scar was on the right-hand cheekbone of the Maharajah.

Bit of a coincidence, but these two obviously weren't the lumps of toadspawn that he and Twinks were looking for. Blotto let the Maharajah and Rani of Pranjipur go on their way.

10

The Message Arrives

The note in Twinks's voice as she addressed her brother was as near to exasperation as she ever allowed it to get. 'But, Blotto, surely you can tell your left from your right?'

'Well, yes, of course I can, Twinks me old banana split.'

'Then why couldn't you see that the mole was on the right side of the woman's chin and the scar was on the man's left cheekbone?'

'Because they weren't. Look.' Blotto raised his right hand and touched the side of his sister's chin. 'That's my right hand—tickey-tockey?'

'Tickey-tockey.'

'So I'm touching the right-hand side of your face.'

'No, Blotto, you're not! You're facing me, so what you're touching is the left-hand side of my face.'

'But when I look in a mirror and touch the right-hand side of my face, that's where I see it.'

'I am not a mirror, Blotto! I'm a real human being, for the love of strawberries!'

'Yes,' he said rather mournfully. He didn't like it when Twinks snapped at him.

'Anyway, given the unusual way in which the couple approached you, you should have been suspicious even if the mole and the scar did seem to be on the wrong sides of their faces.'

'I did think it was a coincidence,' said Blotto in

mitigation.

He looked so pitiful, so eager to please, that, as ever, Twinks found it impossible to stay angry with him. 'Don't worry about it, Blotters. At least we know that the pair who snaffled our Ruperts are still in Paris. And if they think they can get a ransom from us, they may not bother to find a buyer for the paintings.'

'But we aren't going to pay the stenchers any ransom, are we, Twinks?'

'Of course we're not. But we can play them along by pretending we're going to.'

'Good ticket!' A smile spread slowly across Blotto's angelic features. 'I say, a thought's just boffed me on the bonce.'

'What?'

'Well, Twinks me old cheese-grater, if I have, sort of, by chance found the couple who stole the Ruperts . . .'

'Or allowed them to find you.'

'Yes. Well, if I have, that means you no longer have to keep doing your modelling for Blocque and Tacquelle, do you?'

'Oh.' His sister looked slightly put out by the suggestion.

'What's up? What's put lumps in your custard, me old woodlouse?'

'Well . . .' Twinks blushed prettily. (Mind you, she did everything prettily.) 'They are putting a lot of effort into their paintings. It'd be a pity if all of their hard work was sluiced out of the bilges.'

Blotto looked at her in some puzzlement. This was unlike Twinks. In spite of having a lot to boast about—her beauty, her intellect and every other desirable quality in a woman—he had never met one of her gender who had less vanity. Was it possible that even Twinks was attracted by the idea of her body being immortalized as the *chef d'oeuvre* of the *Trianguliste* Movement? Had his sister got one of those things like that classical boddo he'd been told about in Latin lessons at Eton? Apollo, was it? Had even Twinks got an Apollo's heel?

The embarrassed speed with which she changed the subject suggested that he might be on the right track. 'Anyway,' she said, 'award yourself a rosette for making contact with the Vicomte and Vicomtesse de Sales-Malincourt—or the Maharajah and Rani of Pranjipur, but I think I should still follow up my enquiries with Blocque and Tacquelle. We don't want our investigation only to have one prong.'

'Fair biddles,' Blotto agreed, storing away the notion of his sister's vanity for possible use at a later date. 'But what do we do now, Twinks me old carpet-beater?'

'The pair of thimble-jigglers you met said they'd send a message to you here at the Hôtel de Crillon. We await that message.'

Because Blotto and Twinks were the kind of people to whom that kind of thing happened, her words were followed immediately by a tap on the door of their suite. It was a footman bearing a message on a silver salver.

'That was as quick as a cheetah on spikes,' observed Blotto, handing the envelope to his sister as soon as the footman had left the suite.

'But it's for you,' said Twinks, handing it back.

'What?' But sure enough, the missive was addressed: 'PRIVATE—TO BE OPENED

ONLY BY THE HONOURABLE DEVEREUX LYMINSTER'.

'But I haven't got any secrets from you, Twinks. You can read anything that's been sent to me.'

'It might be from some breathsapper of a Frenchwoman who has seen you pongling along the Champs Élysées and fallen for you like a partridge full of lead.'

'Don't talk such toffee, Twinks! I'll bet it's from the Maharajah and Rani of Pranjipur, and its contents are for both of us.'

'You check the SP. I won't look.'

So while Twinks averted her eyes, Blotto opened the envelope.

It wasn't from the Maharajah and Rani of Pranjipur. There were a couple of sheets of paper handwritten in French, with a note on the front which read:

Blotto, I was worried that if I gave this directly to Twinks, she might ignore it like she did the last one. Could you find a subtle way of getting this to her, so that she doesn't realize that it's actually come from me? Relying on you to be a Grade A foundation stone, Buzzer.

Oh, for the love of strawberries, it was another poem from the lovesick Marquis of Bluntleigh! And, to compound the felony, written in French. 'Nothing urgent,' said Blotto, shoving envelope and contents into his pocket.

'Well, I do hope we get the message from the art thieves soon,' said Twinks.

This time her wish was granted. An immediate tap on the door admitted a footman with a message on a silver salver. (He was possibly the same footman who had brought the missive from the Marquis of Bluntleigh, could even have been the same one who had brought the research documents from Professor Erasmus Holofernes, but Blotto and Twinks didn't notice that. People of their breeding paid no more attention to the bearer of a message than they did to the envelope that contained it.)

It was addressed to both of them. Brother and sister pored over the contents.

If you weesh to undertake subtle negotiations concerning zee purchase of zee Tawcester Towers Gainsborough and Reynolds, zee Hon. Lyminster should appear in zee South Tower of zee Cathedral of Notre-Dame near zee Emmanuel Bell at nine o'clock zees evening. Zee Hon. Lyminster should be alone—any attempt to appear wiz anozzer person will mean that no negotiations or meeting will take place. Zee larger key in zees envelope opens zee small door at zee foot of zee South Tower, zee smaller one gives access to zee stairs leading up to zee Bell Tower. If you ever weesh to see your paintings again, follow zee instructions in zees message.

'Larksissimo!' said Twinks. 'This is just the thing to light the fireworks of fun!'

Blotto looked puzzled. 'Who do you think it's addressed to?'

'Well, me obviously.'

'Are you sure it's not me?'

'Why should it be?'

'Well, the poor thimbles who wrote this clearly aren't very good at English, but I'd have thought that "zee Hon. Lyminster" could be meant to mean "the Honourable Lyminster"—or, more correctly, "the Honourable Devereux Lyminster"—in other words, me.'

'But, Blotto me old grapefruit-slicer, couldn't "zee Hon. Lyminster" also be an abbreviation for "zee Honoria Lyminster"—in other words, me.'

Her brother looked perplexed. 'Well, how for the love of strawberries are we supposed to know which one they mean?'

'There is a clue in the message.'

'Is there?'

'They say they want to "undertake subtle negotiations".'

Twinks didn't have to say any more. Her brother knew where his strengths lay, and none of them ever lay in a sentence containing the word 'subtle'. He agreed that it was his sister who was being summoned to the South Tower of Notre-Dame.

'But why do they want you to be on your own?' he asked.

'Perhaps they think,' she chuckled, 'that it'll be easier to deal with a poor little violet of the female persuasion. Perhaps they think I'm a soft centre.'

Her brother laughed at the incongruity of this idea. Anyone who thought they could run circles round Twinks needed a bit of a spring-clean in the brainbox department.

Another thought struck him. 'You don't think it's a trap, do you?'

'Even more grandissimo if it is! I love traps as much as a pike loves troutlings. I love the challenge of the things!'

Blotto smiled proudly. She was quite a girl, his sister.

*   *   *

Since her appointment at Notre-Dame was not till the evening, Twinks went off for her afternoon session of sitting for Eugène Blocque. She was slightly defensive when she told her brother of her plans and Blotto's impression was confirmed that she really did have an ambition to be immortalized as the muse (he understood the word now, knew it was nothing to do with stables) of *Triangulisme*.

He stayed in their suite. Dashed comfortable, the Crillon, and although there were lots of things to be seen in Paris, his morning at the Louvre had provided Blotto with all the sight-seeing he needed for the next few millennia. An innocent snooze on his soft goose-feather bed sounded a lot more attractive as a proposition.

As soon as he lay down, he switched off like a light. Blotto never had any trouble sleeping. He didn't normally do it during the day, but then there were very few days when he'd spent the morning looking at large paintings. An ordeal like that would make any boddo sleepy.

He hadn't undressed for his snooze by more than removing a blazer. Which was just as well, because when he woke up there was a woman in his room!

Not just any woman either. It was Dimpsy Wickett-Coote. And in her eye was a gleam, a gleam he had witnessed in other women's eyes, a gleam that always spelled danger. Dimpsy had amorous intentions towards him.

'Good afternoon, Blotto,' she breathed.

91

'Good afternoon, me old stumps and bails,' he said, trying to bring a quality of levity to the occasion.

She looked down at him from her great height. And she did actually lick her lips.

Blotto felt totally naked without his blazer, but as he half rose from the bed to reach it, a strong hand pushed him back on to the goosedown and, in what seemed to be the same movement, Dimpsy Wickett-Coote was suddenly lying alongside him. Her ardent black eyes burned into his vacant blue ones.

'I see hidden depths in you, Blotto,' she susurrated.

'No, there aren't any,' he protested. 'Shallow as a puddle when the sun comes out, that's me.'

'Blotto,' she murmured, 'I have had many lovers.'

'Toad-in-the-hole . . .' seemed an appropriate response to this, so that was what he said. The next essential, though, was a change of subject, something that got her off the topic of her lovers. So Blotto asked, 'How did you manage to get in here?'

'I have very good connections at the Crillon. The Deputy Under Manager is one of my lovers.'

As a ploy for getting her off the subject of lovers that approach was clearly not going to win any rosettes, so Blotto tried another diversionary tactic. Cricket, he'd found, was always good in these circumstances. Nothing seemed so to dampen a woman's amorous intentions as talk of cricket. So he asked, 'Any idea how England are doing in the Test Match?'

'They're 211 for 3 at stumps in Melbourne,' she replied.

'Well, I'll be snickered,' said Blotto. 'How on earth do you know?'

'The England captain telephoned me the score.'

'Why on earth did the old greengage do that?'

'He is one of my lovers,' replied Dimpsy Wickett-Coote.

Blotto's attempts at getting her off the subject of her lovers seemed to be falling at every fence. Before his brain had time to devise yet another devious ploy, he found his face seized in Dimpsy's hands and his lips pulled towards hers.

'And now you are about to become one of my lovers too,' she murmured ominously.

'I'd be frightfully careful if I were you,' he remonstrated. 'I've got a real stencher of a cold.'

'What do you think I care about a cold, Blotto? I don't give a tailor's tuppence for infectious diseases. After all, I've been spending jeroboamsfuls of time sitting for Blocque and Tacquelle in their studios, and they've got more than colds. They've got the *phtisie*.' Then inevitably she added, 'They're both my lovers.'

'Yes, um, Dimpsy, it seems to me that when it comes to lovers, you've got quite a full dance card. And a girl doesn't want too much mustard on her ham, does she? You know, there is an old tag about having too much of a good thing.'

'But it depends how good the thing of which you have too much is. I am a connoisseur of lovers, Blotto. When I am with the right lover, I become the most beautiful woman in the world.'

'What, like old Blocque and Tacquelle thought you were?'

'Yes.' A shadow crossed her exquisite brow. '*But they no longer think that. Since your sister arrived in Paris.*' There was real venom in the words. 'So now I need a new lover to make me feel once again that I am the most beautiful woman in the world. And I have decided that that lover is going to be you, Blotto.'

He shrank inwardly. Talk of that kind always brought him out in crimps. Oh, what a gluepot, he thought miserably. He never liked being on the horns of a dilemma and Dimpsy Wickett-Coote had just impaled him on a spoffing great big one. They were both already compromised. She, an unmarried woman, was in the hotel bedroom of him an unmarried man.

If someone found them together, in very short order they would be ruined—or married, which was probably worse. Apart from anything else, he didn't think the Dowager Duchess would approve of Dimpsy Wickett-Coote as a daughter-in-law. The purchase of a life peerage was the kind of vulgarity that could be ignored in the father of a schoolfriend. In the father of a potential entrant to the Lyminster family it would become a much whiffier slice of Stilton.

Blotto knew that what he should do was show Dimpsy the door, before any more damage was done. But *noblesse oblige* and all that rombooley . . . His instincts as a gentleman told him he should come up with some honeyed words that would effect the siren's eviction without hurting her feelings. And Blotto had never been very good at coming up with honeyed words.

'Erm, actually . . .' he said, 'when it comes to being a lover and that kind of thing, I think you might find me a bit of an empty revolver. I'm sure you could do better.'

94

'I'll be the judge of that,' replied Dimpsy, in a voice whose forcefulness reminded Blotto uncomfortably of his mother.

'But I'm not sure that—'

'Stop gabbing, Blotto, and kiss me!'

The gentle hold she had on his face had become a vice-like grip. Their lips were almost touching when he had a really beezer brainwave. Rolling out of Dimpsy's clutches, Blotto managed to reach his blazer. Wearing it he felt twice the man he had before as, reaching into its pocket, he produced the Marquis of Bluntleigh's poem. Cunningly he didn't bring out the envelope addressed to Twinks.

'Dimpsy!' he cried rather magnificently. 'Much as I am honoured by the fact that you wish to be my lover, it is a gift which I cannot accept while I know that another man—a friend of mine, in fact, and a far worthier man than I will ever be—loves you far more truly than I ever can. See, he has written this poem for you!' Theatrically, he thrust the paper towards her. 'And what's more, to show how much he loves you, he has written it in French!'

Dimpsy took the poem and glanced at it. 'This is written by Buzzer Bluntleigh.'

'He it is that loves you!'

'No, he doesn't. This poem's addressed to Twinks.'

'What makes you think that?'

'The fact that I helped him write it.'

Oh, broken biscuits, thought Blotto. I'd forgotten that. As it turned out, his really beezer brainwave hadn't been a brainwave at all. Not even a brainripple.

'Now kiss me!' Dimpsy Wickett-Coote

commanded him.

Reluctantly, his stock of escape plans exhausted, Blotto moved towards her. He tried to remember how he'd dug himself out of similar gluepots in the past and suddenly an idea lumbered into his brain. Prayer!

Prayer, and almost inevitably that would involve God. They were neither of them concepts that frequently came into the mind of the Honourable Devereux Lyminster. He didn't really have a faith, as such. Well, he was Church of England, which came to the same thing.

But, as he had once before in a comparable predicament, he found himself praying to someone or something to get him out of the amorous clutches of Dimpsy Wickett-Coote.

And once again it worked!

There was a tap at the bedroom door. Almost weak with relief, Blotto bellowed out, 'Come in!'

And there in the doorway stood Corky Froggett.

11

A Case of Sabotage?

'If it had not been a matter of urgency, milord, I would not have troubled you.' As ever, the chauffeur stood to attention in his uniform, as if he had never left the army. 'I apologize, milord. I did not know you had company.'

'Don't don your worry-boots about that, Corky.' Bizarrely, Blotto found himself about to offer some spurious explanation for Dimpsy's presence in his bedroom, that she'd come to measure him for a pair of sock-suspenders or something of the sort. But then he remembered who he was talking to. Despite their closeness, Corky Froggett was still only a servant, after all. And people of Blotto's class didn't have to explain themselves to servants.

Anyway, his prayer to someone or something had worked. Dimpsy Wickett-Coote was no longer in his bedroom. Blotto wondered whether Corky Froggett had just been spirited there by divine intervention, or whether the chauffeur actually had a reason for appearing at his door. 'So what's the bizz-buzz?' he asked.

'I have reason to believe, milord, that you have been the victim of attempted sabotage.'

'Well, yes, I agree that it was rather a close call with Dimpsy Wickett—'

'No, milord. I refer to the attempted sabotage of your lordship's Lagonda.'

'What!' The colour drained from Blotto's face. It was as if someone had threatened his precious cricket bat . . . or Mephistopheles. 'What's the damage?' he asked tersely.

'Fortunately none, milord . . .' The chauffeur coughed quietly before continuing, 'thanks to my vigilance.'

'You're not a man, you're a god, Corky! Tell me what happened.'

'Well, milord, as you know, I am not billeted here in the Hôtel de Crillon.'

'Yes, hope the gaff they've put you up in ticks the clock for you.'

'It is perfectly adequate, milord . . . for someone of my standing. I have encountered the odd bug in the bed, the sanitary arrangements are of the

"Crouch and Hope" variety, and the food is very . . . er, French, but these privations count as nothing against the knowledge that I am serving you, milord.'

'Good ticket, Corky. Hope you haven't been bitten too much by the little pinkers.'

'No, milord. I have fortunately not been attacked by the bed bugs . . . because I have not been sleeping in the bed.'

'Why not, for the love of strawberries?'

'Milord, during the last major European dust-up, I fought in France.'

'I know you did, Corky. And bear the scars to prove it.'

'Yes, milord. And I have no regrets about any of those scars . . . or indeed about any of the large number of enemy soldiers I was fortunate enough to kill.'

'Hoopee-doopee, Corky.'

'However, milord, in the course of that conflict, I did find myself in close proximity to many representatives of the French soldiery.'

'Well, you would have done. You were on the same side as them.'

Corky Froggett's upper lip curled, also curling the white moustache that stood to attention above it. 'Yes, on the same side, but with rather different priorities.'

'Oh?'

'The fact is, milord, that no French soldier will ever have the fighting qualities of his English equivalent.'

'Well, of course they won't, Corky. That's been common knowledge for centuries. Ancestor of mine made the same observation at Agincourt.'

'Yes . . .' The chauffeur was silent for a moment. 'Not to put too fine a point on it, milord, I don't trust the French.'

'Very right and proper, Corky.'

'So for that reason I have not been sleeping in the accommodation provided for me by the Hôtel de Crillon . . . preferring to make up my camp bed down in the hotel's garages . . . where I can keep an eye on your lordship's Lagonda.'

'Good thinking, Corky. You're a Grade A foundation stone.'

'The vehicle is safe during the day, milord, because a lot of mechanics and chauffeurs are coming and going, but I had a hunch it needed guarding through the hours of darkness.'

'And did your hunch prove correct?'

'I'm afraid it did, milord. Last night, I regret to say, at about three in the morning I was guilty of falling asleep.'

'Don't boff yourself on the bonce about that, Corky. We all need our snore-time.'

'Yes, the fact is, I had perhaps been over-enjoying the pleasures of Paris. But I swear I only slept for a few moments, milord.'

'On the garage floor was this?'

'No, milord. On the back seat of the Lagonda.' And, in case this might be regarded as a form of *lèse-majesté* towards the car, the chauffeur was quick to explain, 'After considerable experimentation, I found that to be the optimum position for surveillance, milord. Were I on the garage floor or in the front seat, I might have been seen by potential malefactors and thus frightened them off . . . whereas from the back seat I would be in the perfect location to surprise anyone who entered through the driver's door of the Lagonda—and garotte them.'

'Good ticket, Corky.'

'And I was indeed woken from my brief slumber by the sound of someone getting into the car.'

'The stencher!' said Blotto. 'Was he trying to steal it?'

'I don't believe so, milord. I think, as I mentioned earlier, their intention was sabotage.'

'"Their"? You mean there was more than one of the lumps of toadspawn?'

'There were two. And they displayed striking ignorance of the specifications of the Lagonda. In fact, milord, I would go so far as to say that they'd never seen one before.'

'How so?'

'They clearly had no knowledge of how to open the car's bonnet.'

'Didn't they? What pot-brained pineapples!'

'I thought exactly the same myself, milord. The little rat who entered the car did so in the belief that there might be some bonnet release on the inside.'

Master and servant both had a good laugh at that, before Blotto asked, 'So why did they want to get inside the bonnet of the Lag?'

'One of the lily-livered cheesemongers had a pair of metal snips with him. It is my belief that he planned to cut through the Lagonda's brake cables.'

'The four-faced thimble-jiggler!' cried Blotto. It wasn't his habit to use such strong language, but when someone threatened his Lag . . . well, he felt rather the way a mother sheep is reputed to feel towards her ewe lamb.

'I did of course frustrate their schemes. Suddenly making my presence known, I was able to surprise the bounder inside the car—though sadly he managed to wriggle out of my grasp before I could garotte him.'

'Oh well, you can't have everything, Corky. And it may have been for the best. Explaining a garotted corpse in the garage of the Hôtel de Crillon might prompt a few awkward questions for you from the local *gendarmerie*.'

'Yes, milord, but that wouldn't worry me. You know I'd be happy to go to the gallows, so long as I was doing it in your service.'

'What a Grade A foundation stone you are, Corky. But, by the way, I've a feeling they don't have gallows here in France. They use the . . . what's the word? Guillemot?'

'I think you will find, milord, with respect, that the guillemot is a kind of seabird.'

'Is it, by Denzil?'

'I believe so, milord. The French device used for the meting out of capital punishment is called the *guillotine*.' A note of awe came into Corky Froggett's voice as he continued, 'A very fine piece of engineering, milord. Possibly the most efficient and finest method of ending a man's life. Were the local *gendarmerie* to arrest me for the garotting of someone in the garage of the Hôtel de Crillon, I would regard it as an honour to be decapitated by a machine as fine as the *guillotine*.'

'Well, that just shows what a fine block of English granite you are, Corky. Fortunately, however, you didn't manage to garotte anyone in the garage of the Hôtel de Crillon, so you're currently not on any decapitation list.'

'No.' The chauffeur could not keep an edge of disappointment out of his voice. His main aspiration, the fulfilment of his whole life, would be that moment when he was allowed to lay down his life for his young master. It wasn't a matter of whether that event happened, it was simply a matter of when. But clearly, for the time being, the apotheosis of Corky Froggett was deferred.

'Anyway, did you get a look at these stenchers? Would you recognize them again? If they were in an identity parade?'

'They were very distinctive figures, milord. Notable chiefly for their height.'

'Tall boddos, eh?'

'No, milord. Rather the reverse. They were both of very diminutive stature.'

'How diminutive?'

'Neither of them would have come up any higher than my waist.'

'Toad-in-the-hole!'

'It is to that fact that I put down my failure to garotte the one inside the car. His neck was rather lower down in the seat than I had anticipated.'

'Never mind, Corky. You can't win a coconut every time.'

'That, milord, is sadly true.'

Blotto was thoughtful. 'They really are masters of disguise, you know.'

'I'm sorry, milord. I do not know to whom you are referring.'

'The couple who snaffled the Ruperts from Tawcester Towers. Disguised then as the Vicomte and Vicomtesse de Sales-Malincourt. Disguised when I met them this morning as the Maharajah and Rani of Pranjipur. And disguised in the early

102

hours of last night in the garage here as a pair of midgets. As I say, they really are masters of disguise.'

Corky Froggett was about to say he thought it unlikely that a normal-sized man and woman could pass themselves off as two male midgets, but he thought better of it. He was wary of uttering anything that might be construed as criticism of his master.

'Anyway,' said Blotto, 'nice innings, Corky. You saved the Lag, so give that pony a rosette.'

'Thank you very much, milord.'

'Erm . . . one thing?'

'Yes, milord?'

'You spoke a few minutes back of "over-enjoying the pleasures of Paris" . . .'

'I did indeed, milord, and I apologize for taking advantage of—'

'No, don't worry about that, Corky. All I want to know is: are there any "pleasures of Paris"?'

'Undoubtedly, milord.'

'Because I'm afraid I haven't come across them. Well, I suppose the wine's tolerable, but they ruin all the food by smothering it with sauces. Then they add this filth-fingering guff called garlic to everything. And I went to a swamphole this morning called the Louvre which had nothing in it but spoffing great paintings. I mean, what do people come here to Paris for?'

'A lot of people come for the nightlife, milord.'

'"Nightlife"? Have you been enjoying the nightlife, Corky?'

'I have to confess I have.'

'What, lying on the garage floor of the—?'

'No, milord.' Then, thinking this might suggest

103

some dereliction of his duty, the chauffeur quickly asserted that, though he had spent much of his time in the garage, he had also managed to fit in a few hours of nightlife.

'So what is the attraction of the nightlife?'

Corky Froggett coughed discreetly before replying, 'The women, milord.'

'Women?'

'Paris is famous for its women, milord.'

Blotto looked puzzled. 'But I don't seem to have seen any more women in Paris than one might in London.'

'It is not the number of women that distinguishes Paris, milord, it is their nature. English women in my experience, milord, lack a certain generosity . . .'

'Do they? I wouldn't have said that. I mean, the mater always stumps up some kind of present for me at Christmas, pair of socks, that kind of rombooley, and I—'

'No, milord. I was referring to generosity of a more . . . intimate nature.' Blotto looked totally bewildered. 'Paris is the home of the *poule de luxe*.'

Blotto's brow cleared. 'Oh yes, I think I had that in the restaurant downstairs. Again, covered with far too many sauces and that ghastly garlic and—'

'No, milord, I am speaking of a . . . "lady of the night". Do you understand that expression?'

'Of course. I had one at Tawcester Towers.'

'Did you, milord?' This was opening up a whole new dimension in the chauffeur's knowledge of his master's character.

'Yes. Mind you, she was called a night nurse. And I was very young at the time.'

'Ah.'

'Anyway, Corky, do you think I should have a go at this nightlife business then?'

'It would be a pity for any gentleman to come to Paris without tasting it, milord.'

'Then taste it I shall. When shall I start?'

'Will you be free this evening, milord?'

Blotto thought about it. It was that evening that Twinks was busy with her rendezvous (and possible entrapment) at Notre-Dame. 'Yes, of course I'm free.'

'In that case, milord, I will have pleasure in driving you in the Lagonda to Montmartre . . . where I will introduce you to the delights of . . . the Folies Bergère!'

12

A Dangerous Rendezvous

Larksissimo, thought Twinks as she crossed the Pont Neuf on her way to the Île de la Cité. She couldn't help admitting to herself that she was enjoying sitting for Blocque and Tacquelle, and she knew she was enjoying it for all the wrong reasons. For one of the rare occasions in his life, Blotto had been right. The idea of being immortalized as the muse of the *chef d'oeuvre* of the *Tringuliste* Movement had really fired her ambition.

Because, if you were the Right Honourable Honoria Lyminster, daughter of the Duke and Duchess of Tawcester, brought up at Tawcester Towers, you didn't really have many ambitions.

Some girls in her situation might have wished that they were more beautiful, but without false modesty Twinks knew she was the most beautiful woman in the world. Some might have wished for greater sporting prowess, but Twinks knew she could beat anyone at any game they chose to challenge her at. Some might have wished for greater bravery, but Twinks didn't know the meaning of the word fear. (This was something she had in common with her brother. Mind you, there were quite a lot of words Blotto didn't know the meaning of.)

And when it came to brainpower . . . well, actually very few girls of Twinks's upbringing would have been too bothered about that, but she was quietly confident that the world boasted very few people who could match her intellectual capacity. Professor Erasmus Holofernes might possibly have the edge on her there, but then he'd had the advantage of an education at most of the world's best universities, whereas Twinks was self-taught. She had had a sequence of governesses when she was a child at Tawcester Towers, but in most cases she ended up teaching them. And she'd done the same to the nuns at St Wilhelmina's.

The other thing that preoccupied the ambitions of many girls was men. To feel fulfilled they needed to know they could inspire blind adoration in the male gender. But there again, Twinks had grown up secure in the knowledge that a man had no more than to look at her before he began protesting his undying love. Indeed, the exception would be the man who didn't immediately fall for her like an anchor from a liner.

So it was hardly surprising that a young woman

so starved of unrealized ambitions should be attracted by the idea of gaining enduring fame as an artist's muse.

As to which artist it was, she didn't mind. Blocque and Tacquelle seemed to her to be almost interchangeable as personalities. They both still coughed a lot as they transformed her contours into triangles, and neither would let any of their sessions end without another attempt to lure her into his unsavoury bed. But she could brush off such advances with ease—as she had brushed off so many before them.

Anyway, having the two of them working on rival portrayals of her she thought of as a kind of insurance policy. Posterity could decide whether it was Blocque or Tacquelle who had produced the *chef d'oeuvre* of the *Trisanguliste* Movement. Either way the subject would be her.

So Twinks had no desire to leave Paris until the paintings were both finished. She did feel marginally guilty about this. She knew she should be concentrating on the investigation that she and Blotto had taken on. She could no longer convince herself that she was actually getting useful information from Blocque and Tacquelle about the criminal side of the Parisian art world.

Still, in his own idiosyncratic way, Blotto was getting somewhere. Though his encounter with the Maharajah and Rani of Pranjipur had been engineered by them rather than him, it had at least advanced the investigation. Finally they were making progress. The message had duly come to the Hôtel de Crillon, which was why Twinks was on her way to Notre-Dame, walking into what was almost certainly a trap.

107

What more could a girl want than to be on her way, protected only by her silver-fox-fur coat and the contents of her reticule, to a rendezvous at the top of a tall building with people of criminal—and very possibly homicidal—tendencies? Yes, the whole situation was pure creamy éclair. Once again Twinks thought to herself, larksissimo.

The larger key had no problem opening the small door at the foot of Notre-Dame's South Tower. She didn't relock it, covering herself in case she needed a quick getaway. The vast interior of the cathedral was spectrally quiet. If there was anyone inside, they were not drawing attention to themselves. The only light came from some votive candles that had been lit to expiate God alone knew what sins committed by the citizens of Paris.

On another occasion Twinks would have paused to take in the beauties of the spectacular vaulted interior. Unlike her brother, she did have a refined appreciation of the arts. But that particular evening there were more pressing demands on her time.

The smaller key also did its business and, leaving the second door unlocked as well, Twinks was soon climbing up a narrow spiral staircase. She had contemplated leaving the door open to let in some light, but decided that might alert any nightwatchmen (assuming the cathedral employed some). Anyway, an open door would only have illuminated the first few steps before they twisted away into the darkness above. The air in the staircase was very cold. She wrapped her silver fox fur around her.

Twinks kept her right hand against the cold stone of the wall as she corkscrewed her way upwards.

The only sound, unnaturally loud in her head, was the slight rasp of her own breathing. The steps and the darkness seemed to go on for ever.

Just as she was beginning to feel she must be higher than the tip of Notre-Dame's topmost extremity, she was aware of a slight glow of light above her. As she climbed closer, it grew brighter. Still not bright, it was only candlelight, but brighter.

She emerged on to a narrow wood-floored gallery, which ran all the way round the interior of the tower-top. The thirteen-ton bulk of the Emmanuel bourdon bell loomed beside her.

But she had no eyes for bells, no eyes for anything except what she saw in the corner ahead of her. Propped casually against the wall, illuminated by two candles in holders in front of them, stood the two Ruperts. She had found the Tawcester Towers Gainsborough and Reynolds! Mission accomplished!

But stepping forward towards the prize, Twinks felt the wooden floor beneath her give. As her arms flailed against emptiness, her only thought was that she hadn't been just the victim of a trap, but also of a trapdoor.

13

Les Folies Bergère

The two midgets the other side of the gallery looked round the great bell at the hanging flap of the trapdoor. 'No one can survive a fall like that,' observed one. In French.

'No,' agreed the other. 'We have done what La Puce requires.'

'Do we remove the body?'

'No. We had no instructions to do that. When she is found in the morning it will be reported just as the death of another over-enthusiastic tourist.'

'And do we remove the paintings?'

'Were we instructed to remove the paintings?'

'No.'

'Then we do not remove them. When one is working for La Puce one does what is demanded of one—and nothing else! La Puce has no admiration for people who think for themselves.'

'Very good. So our job here is done.'

'It certainly is. Another triumph for . . . *les rats de Paris*!'

And they both let out evil laughs. In French, of course.

*　　*　　*

Blotto wasn't quite sure what he was expecting from the Folies Bergère. It was also rather strange to be going out with Corky Froggett in a social context. In fact, it would be quite a hoot to tell some of his Old Etonian muffin-toasters that he had gone out for an evening of entertainment with his chauffeur! Toad-in-the-hole, how times were changing. Next thing Blotto could find himself being accused of having Socialist leanings!

(Only as a joke, of course—nobody would really imagine that he had any time for such filthy doctrines. Some of those Socialist stenchers even went as far as recommending the abolition of the aristocracy! What a pot-brained notion! If that sort of thing was allowed to happen in England, the country might end up like . . . well, like France. Blotto shuddered at the very idea.)

The first thing he noticed at the Folies Bergère was that there did seem to be a lot of women around—and this was even before the stage show started. What's more, the women around the Folies Bergère weren't the kind that Blotto was used to encountering. They were exotically caparisoned and there was something funny about the front of their dresses. Had Blotto known the word, he would have recognized the phenomenon as *décolletage*, but he didn't. All that flesh was, however, a sight he had rarely seen. Well, a boddo wouldn't if he'd been brought up at Tawcester Towers and educated at Eton.

So he just thought the women were in danger of catching their deaths of cold when they went outside. Maybe it was a function of poverty, he reasoned. The women could not afford quite enough of the lavish silks and velvets of their dresses to cover up the front bit. If so, he felt very sorry for the poor pineapples . . . talk about spoiling the ship for a ha'porth of tar. He even had the gallant, charitable thought that he should offer one of them his opera cloak, but there were so many that charity to one individual might be in danger of being interpreted by the others as favouritism.

The other striking thing about the women was how friendly they were. Arising from a history that went back to Agincourt and Crécy—and probably a lot further—Blotto had somehow got it into his mind that the French were a standoffish nation, given to frequent shrugging and reacting to most overtures with a dismissive *'pouf'* sound.

But not a bit of it at the Folies Bergère. The women were almost excessively affable. They seemed delighted to see him and though he couldn't understand most of what they were saying, they were apparently offering all kinds of delightful things. The only word he could catch in their cascade of French was *'milord'*. He was quite impressed that they'd got that right. Must be something about his bearing, he decided, that singled him out as a member of the aristocracy. Or maybe just his immaculate evening dress, his opera cloak, top hat and silver-topped cane.

But then he heard one of the women calling Corky Froggett *'milord'* as well. At first Blotto thought that rather odd, but then he rationalized it to himself. These women, properly aware of their national inadequacies, recognized that by comparison with the French any Englishman was an aristocrat.

It was also noticeable that Corky seemed to be very well acquainted with some of the women. The chauffeur submitted to a lot of hugging and kissing and ooh-la-la-ing. Some of the giggling suggested that he and the women might have some kind of shared secret. Blotto couldn't for the life of him imagine what that might be.

He ordered champagne and was again struck by how unstandoffish the women were. They seemed quite happy to sit at his and Corky's table and share his wine. As they all waited for the evening's entertainment to begin, Blotto couldn't help observing that a particularly well-upholstered woman had taken a seat beside him and, for some unknown reason, was rubbing her leg against his under the table.

'Good evening, *milord*,' she said.

He good eveninged back.

'My name is Fifi,' she said.

'Ah. Blotto.'

'No, I am not.' She raised her champagne glass. 'Not yet, anyway.' She took a long swallow and smiled at him.

Blotto smiled back, but couldn't think of anything to say. Then remembering his late father the Duke's fall-back question when visiting members of the oikish classes, he asked the woman what she did.

'I am *demimondaine*,' she replied.

'Ah,' said Blotto. 'I'm Church of England.'

Fifi chuckled throatily, and once again Blotto felt the pressure of her leg running up and down his.

'Got a bit of an itch, have you?' he asked.

Fifi's English was good enough in certain specialized areas for her to understand this and she replied, with what Blotto considered to be excessive sultriness, 'I most certainly have, *milord*. Perhaps the *milord* would like to scratch my itch?'

'Frightfully decent of you to offer,' he replied, 'but I think you'll find rubbing it against the table leg does the trick.'

'Ah.'

He thought he detected disappointment in her tone, which was a bit of a rum baba. 'What's the problem, Fifi?' he asked. 'Fleas?'

'Fleece? Like a sheep?'

'No, no, fleas. I thought that your itch might have been caused by fleas.' Her expression remained blank. Sultry, but blank. Blotto looked round the table for support. 'Any of you breathsappers know what the French is for a flea?'

'*Une puce,*' said one of the women.

'La Puce,' said another. And at her words a shudder ran round the whole table. Not only their table, but adjacent tables too. Blotto looked around in bewilderment. 'Why's that put lumps in everyone's custard?' he asked.

Who knows whether he might have got an answer? He didn't, though, because at that moment the lights in the great auditorium dimmed and the evening's show began.

Now Blotto wasn't a whale on the theatre. So strong had been his reaction at Eton to being force-fed Shakespeare that he had managed to expunge almost every word of it from his memory. There was one famous bit he recalled which began, 'To be . . .', but he no longer was certain what came next. Somewhere in the recesses of his mind he thought the next words might be 'a pilgrim', but as a bet he wouldn't even have put ten shillings on it.

That unfortunate early experience with Shakespeare had coloured his attitude to the drama in general. On the very few occasions when he hadn't been able to duck going to the theatre,

114

he would have been hard pushed to say whether his dominant feeling was boredom or confusion. One evening he'd inadvertently ended up watching Ibsen, and though the play had been translated into English, it would probably have made rather more sense to him in the original Norwegian. At the end he'd expressed the view that what the characters needed to get them out of their self-absorption was a good day's hunting.

On the other hand, Blotto didn't mind so much going to shows that didn't have a plot to keep up with. A few songs, a bit of dancing, pretty costumes . . . that could make an acceptable filler between cocktails and dinner when he had to leave his precious Tawcester Towers and go up to the metropolis. But experience of London revues hadn't prepared him for the Folies Bergère.

Once again he had the thought that the women on stage must be frightfully cold. And in their case it was hard to explain the skimpiness of the costumes on grounds of poverty, because the inadequate strips of clothing they did wear were highly decorated with spangles and feathers. He wondered whether their mothers knew they were going round dressed like that.

It was also soon evident that a good mother would not have brought up her daughter to dance in the manner that the girls of the Folies Bergère danced. Like all people with narrow horizons, Blotto started a lot of sentences with the line: 'Now I'm as broad-minded as the next boddo . . .', but he would have had to confess to being rather shocked by the routines he witnessed that evening. He'd always made the tacit assumption that girls did have legs, but he'd never imagined that they had as much leg as he witnessed at the Folies Bergère. For most of the show he didn't know where to look.

An academic researching the English class system might have extrapolated some useful data from the occasion. For while Blotto seemed preoccupied with the patent leather of his shoes, the reactions of Corky Froggett were very different. The chauffeur had no problem with where to direct his eyes. Indeed, his manner suggested he wished he'd brought a pair of binoculars. And the eyes which he focused on the stage could only be described as 'pop'. Though Corky's military training prevented him from actually drooling, beneath the stiff moustache his tongue hung like that of a panting Labrador who's just finished chasing a particularly fleet-footed cat.

At the end of the evening's entertainment Blotto felt more confused rather than less. Fascinating though it had been to share his chauffeur's idea of a good night out, he did not think it was an experiment he would care to repeat. He felt suddenly nostalgic for home. How he would have loved to spend that night tucked up in his own bed in his draughty bedroom at Tawcester Towers, with no more challenging prospect for the morning than a day's hunting on his beloved Mephistopheles.

But he had to shake such thoughts out of his head. He and Twinks were on a mission; they could not return to England without the stolen Gainsborough and Reynolds. Idly, Blotto wondered how his sister's visit to Notre-Dame had developed. He felt a little surge of excitement from the idea that she might already have retrieved the stolen goods. Maybe the two Ruperts were, even as he had the thought, safely awaiting him at the Hôtel de Crillon along with Twinks. Maybe they would be able to drive back to Tawcester Towers the following day. He imagined Mephistopheles's whinny of recognition as his master rounded the corner of the stable block.

For some reason, Corky Froggett seemed less keen to leave the Folies Bergère than his master. Indeed, when Blotto said they should be on their way, he saw on his chauffeur's face the nearest approximation he had ever encountered there to insubordination. It was with some reluctance that Corky disentangled himself from one of the inadequately fronted women and set off to find the Lagonda.

As Blotto made to follow him, Fifi laid a hand on his arm, winked at him and said, 'Remember, *milord*, when you wish to scratch my itch you know what to do, don't you?'

He smiled at her and said helpfully, 'My nanny always recommended putting witch hazel on it.'

The night air was cold outside the Folies Bergère, and there were a lot of people milling around, but Corky Froggett had got the Lagonda parked right opposite the entrance. Blotto was surprised to find Fifi still beside him as he left the music hall. Other women clutched at his cloak as he stepped through the throng, but he did not allow himself to be detained and made it to the side of the car just as the chauffeur opened the passenger door for him.

Fortunately, Blotto kept his topper on and had to crouch a little as he climbed into the Lagonda. Otherwise, the bullet that made neat entrance and exit wounds through his hat would have made them through his skull.

Master and chauffeur turned as one towards the sound of the shot. Only a few yards away they saw a midget holding a revolver in his hand. With a cry of something in French, the little man brought the gun barrel in line for another shot at Blotto.

He might have hit his target but for the sixteen stone of aggrieved vassal that hit him in the form of Corky Froggett. The second bullet shot harmlessly up into the Parisian night sky.

The chauffeur had the would-be assassin firmly in his grasp and would have held on, had not a second midget suddenly appeared out of the throng and smashed him over the head with a bludgeon. In the moment Corky's hands flew to his head, the trapped midget broke free and, with more incomprehensible shouts, the two of them vanished into the sea of legs outside the Folies Bergère.

'Are you all right, Corky old warrior?' asked Blotto as he helped the chauffeur into a sitting position.

' 'Course I'm all right, milord. I'll have a bruise the size of an ostrich egg in the morning, and concussion for a few days, I would imagine, but I'm all right.' He tried to stand, but tottered dizzily down again and drifted into oblivion.

As Blotto rose to his feet, he was surprised to find himself wrapped in the voluptuous embrace of Fifi. '*Milord*,' she kept saying, '*milord*, they tried to kill you—the *salauds*!'

'Hello,' said Blotto, who knew the routine by now. 'Do you know who they were?' he asked.

Fifi nodded. 'They are two of many such evil

creatures who are known as *les rats de Paris*!'

' "Rah"?' he echoed. 'As in "Rah-rah"?'

'Rats!' said Fifi.

'Rats! I agree,' said Blotto. 'Damned poor show.'

'No, the dwarves are called the rats of Paris. There are many of them . . . and all of them are in the pay of . . . La Puce!'

Everyone who was within hearing of Fifi, even though they hadn't been listening to her up until that point, shuddered as they heard those two fateful words.

'What was it those rat boddos shouted?' asked Blotto.

'As he fired the first shot, the one with the gun shouted that you should go and join your *soeur*.'

'Oh, that's rather bad form.'

'What is?'

'Well, to call me "sir". Everyone else has got it right and called me "*milord*".'

'No, *milord*, it is "*soeur*" meaning your sister. The *rat de Paris* said you should go and join your sister.'

'Ah,' said Blotto. Then slowly, working it out, he went on, 'And he said that as he was hoping to kill me?'

'Exactly so, *milord*.'

Blotto's mental processes ground on at their customary speed. 'So, if he thought he was killing me and he said I should join my sister . . . what he meant was . . .'

Fifi nodded as Blotto took in the implications of his own words.

'I must get to Notre-Dame!' he cried. 'I must find out what's happened to Twinks!'

14

Twinks in Jeopardy!

Bundling the unconscious Corky Froggett into the back seat, Blotto drove the Lagonda across Paris like a man possessed. And it seemed only a matter of moments before he was on the Île de la Cité and running towards the looming mass of Notre-Dame.

Remembering the instructions in the message delivered to the Hôtel de Crillon, he quickly located the small door in the South Tower and let himself into the cathedral. Some of the votive candles had burnt out since his sister's arrival, but enough light still spilled across the vast space for Blotto to find the second door. The fitness from summers of cricket and winters of hunting stood him in good stead as he ran blindly up the spiral staircase into the darkness above.

When finally he reached the top, he was confronted by the same scene as his sister had been. The two Ruperts, still illuminated by the candles in front of them, were tantalizingly close.

But there was a difference between what Blotto saw in the gallery and what Twinks had seen. Between him and the stolen paintings was a break in the wooden flooring, a void from the far side of which the hinged trapdoor hung downwards.

Even for someone of such glacially slow comprehension as Blotto, it wasn't difficult to piece together what had happened.

What had happened to Twinks.

15

Hanging by a Thread!

Brother and sister had survived many scrapes in the past, and their innate optimism prompted them to look for the best in any predicament. But Blotto was finding it tricky to glean anything good in the depths of the current gluepot.

He blamed himself. Of course he blamed himself. He should have ignored the conditions given in the message they had received at the Hôtel de Crillon. He should never have allowed his sister to go to Notre-Dame on her own.

'Twinks,' he said miserably—and, unknowingly, aloud. 'Twinks! What have I allowed to happen to you?'

His words echoed in the high emptiness of the ancient cathedral. He looked down into the void beneath the open trapdoor. Meagre light from the guttering candles flickered on to monumental pillars and carved saints somehow shrunken in their niches.

He reckoned it was another moment when praying to someone or something might be worth a try. But he didn't try it with much optimism.

And once again his prayer was answered. (A more reflective person than Blotto might have seen a correlation between his praying and his prayers being answered, might even have been converted to belief in an omnipotent deity who could make the world a better place. He might have found faith. But Blotto's mind didn't work like that. He was happy to stay Church of England.)

Not only was his prayer answered, but it was answered by what appeared to be a miracle. A voice emerged from one of the niched saints, crying, 'It's all right, Blotto. Everything's tickey-tockey!'

He looked downwards and detected that, yes, one of the saints looked different from the others. Most were shadowy figures, grey against the prevailing grey of the medieval stonework. But in one niche was a figure outlined in radiant, fuzzy white.

Blotto had not witnessed a miracle before (if you discount the moment when his mother the Dowager Duchess once mistakenly showed him some affection when he was a baby). And he wasn't quite sure about the proper reaction to seeing a stone statue come to life and speak. Kneeling down, though, he reckoned must be the minimum requirement.

But before his knees touched the wooden floor, the magical voice spoke again. 'Don't don your worry-boots, Blotto me old tea caddy,' it said. 'Just get me out of this fumacious swamphole.'

'Twinks . . . ?' asked Blotto, hardly daring to believe that it was really her.

'Yes, of course it's me, you Grade A poodle! You don't think I'd let myself be coffinated by a couple of little stenchers like that.'

'But how did you escape?'

'Time enough for that when you've extracted me from this gluepot.'

'Tickey-tockey, Twinks. And how am I going to do that?'

'I think it's going to have to be the old Quasimodo routine, me old pineapple.'

'Quasi— who?'

Quickly reminding herself that her brother wouldn't have a clue what she was talking about, Twinks explained, 'Swinging from the bell-rope.'

'Ah, read your semaphore. Good ticket.' Blotto was pleased with the idea. He always found physical activity so much easier than the mental kind. With a cry of 'Hoopee-doopee!', he launched himself out to snatch at the rope that hung down from the beam supporting Emmanuel. His weight was sufficient for the great bell to let out a strike that seemed to shatter all the ambient air.

Using the momentum from his leap, Blotto contrived to swing across and grab a jutting cornice of stone on the wall of the tower opposite his sister. Once there, he shifted his grip further down the bell-rope and, kicking off from the stonework, swung across the void to gather Twinks out of her niche and into his arms.

Emmanuel registered the additional weight by tolling again, twice. How this irregular time-keeping might be interpreted by the wakeful citizens of Paris, Blotto and Twinks neither knew nor cared.

Thereafter it was a simple matter for brother and sister to shin up the rope to the safety of the wooden gallery.

'So what happened, Twinks me old fish-slice?' asked Blotto. 'How did you save yourself?'

'Oh, it was all creamy éclair,' replied his sister. 'The trapdoor was obviously set up to get me. I should have been expecting something like that, but I was so keen to retrieve the Ruperts that I wasn't concentrating. All I knew was that suddenly the floor had vanished beneath my feet.'

'With a view to you ending up as a dollop of plum jam on the cathedral floor?'

'Give that pony a rosette! That's exactly the fate those murdey midgets had in mind for me. But of course there was no way I was going to let it happen.'

'Of course not.'

'Well, fortunately, I'm the kind of girl who never goes anywhere without her reticule. And as I felt myself falling, I reached into it and pulled out my housewife.'

'You kept a housewife in there?' asked Blotto, astounded. 'Was this another of the midgets?'

'No, no. I mean "housewife" in the sense of a sewing kit.'

'Oh?' Blotto had never heard the expression (but then there were quite a lot of other expressions he hadn't heard either).

'Anyway, me old banana flambé, I always keep in my housewife a reel of extra-strong silk thread . . . you know, in case a button comes off or I find myself falling from the bell tower of a French cathedral. I permanently have a large loop at the end of the silk and with that I managed, as I fell, to lasso the crozier of the carved bishop in the niche from which you have just rescued me. Easy as a housemaid's virtue,' concluded Twinks, rubbing her hands together with satisfaction.

'I knew I shouldn't have donned my worry-boots about you, Twinks. You always were a Grade A foundation stone.'

'Do me best, Blotters.' She became businesslike. 'Anyway, enough of this guff. What we need to do now is take possession of the Ruperts and pongle off as soon as possible back to Tawcester Towers.'

'Hoopee-doopee!' said Blotto.

'Larksissimo!' said Twinks.

They inspected the trapdoor. Though they could pull it back up into position, the latch that was meant to hold it in place had been permanently damaged by whoever had set the booby-trap for Twinks. The wooden floor once again looked intact, but the slightest weight would take the flap down again. So rather than going straight to the Gainsborough and Reynolds, brother and sister edged the long way round three sides of the gallery to rescue the stolen paintings.

Their view of the top of the spiral staircase was impeded by the huge bulk of Emmanuel when they heard approaching footsteps and voices. Blotto couldn't understand what was being said.

'They're speaking French,' his sister murmured.

'The stenchers!' he murmured back.

'In fact,' Twinks went on, 'I recognize their voices. They're the Vicomte and Vicomtesse de Sales-Malincourt.'

'Or the Maharajah and Rani of Pranjipur,' hissed Blotto.

'Exactly.' Twinks listened. 'They're saying they want to get the paintings before they are taken by La Puce.'

Blotto chuckled softly. 'Or rather by us,' he said.

Brother and sister were by now far enough round the great bell to see the approaching couple, currently disguised as a Catholic priest and a nun. They were far enough round also to see the pair spot the Tawcester Towers paintings and hurry towards them.

125

But as soon as the combined weight of the thieves landed on the trapdoor, the inevitable happened. The flap dropped open, the pair vanished and the only thing left of them was the echo of their screams high in the vaulting of Notre-Dame.

Blotto and Twinks exchanged looks but made no comment as they moved towards their goal. But to their amazement, just as they were almost close enough to touch the paintings, the Gainsborough and the Reynolds rose up in front of them. Candlelight caught on the thin wires by which they had been suspended, and by which they were now being lifted up to the top of the South Tower.

It was a matter of moments for Blotto to find the narrow staircase that led up to the cathedral's roof. When he reached it, thin moonlight washed over the night-time Paris that was spread out before him.

And he could see, moving away from Notre-Dame in a southerly direction, a hot-air balloon, in whose gondola, he felt certain, were stashed the Tawcester Towers' Gainsborough and Reynolds.

16

Back at Les Deux Mangetouts

Dimpsy Wickett-Coote was rather enjoying herself at Les Deux Mangetouts. She thrived on masculine attention, and on this occasion she was the focus of four men's interest. Drinking *absinthe* with her into the small hours were Eugène Blocque, Gaston

Tacquelle, Chuck Waggen, Scott Frea and the Marquis of Bluntleigh.

Now obviously, after their bonding at St Wilhelmina's, Twinks remained her best friend, but Dimpsy was finding an evening away from her best friend had quite a lot to be said for it. Men, she had always found, lacked imagination and, without actually having the most beautiful woman in the world present, were prepared to find beauty in whoever they happened to be with. Which that evening was her, Dimpsy Wickett-Coote.

It helped her cause that there were long-standing rivalries between the two *Triangulistes*, and also between the two American writers. Any woman on whom Eugène Blocque cast a lascivious eye automatically became the object of Gaston Tacquelle's equally lascivious attentions. Exactly the same competitive spirit dominated the relationship between Chuck Waggen and Scott Frea.

Only the Marquis of Bluntleigh remained morosely aware of the absence of his beloved Twinks. But four out of five men paying court to her was, thought Dimpsy, not a bad percentage.

'Perhaps I will return to painting your portrait, Dimpsy,' said Eugène Blocque, before being overtaken by a bout of coughing. 'I am sorry, it is the *phtisie*.'

Gaston Tacquelle took up the challenge. 'I will definitely return to painting you, Dimpsy,' he announced before he too succumbed to the *phtisie*. 'And what is more . . .' he said when he'd recovered sufficiently to get words out, 'I am nearer to death than that charlatan, that *malade imaginaire*, Eugène Blocque.'

This is very promising, thought Dimpsy. Always a good sign when the two *Trianguliste*s started competitive coughing.

'Just a cotton-picking minute,' Chuck Waggen interrupted. 'Your painting stinks. All triangles. What use are they? Dimpsy deserves better. I'll put her in my next book.'

'No,' said Scott Frea, picking up the challenge. 'I'll put her in *my* next book.'

'My book will be better than yours.'

'My book will be more sensitive than yours.'

'Being in my book will make Dimpsy famous!'

'Being in my book will make her even more famous!'

'Being in my painting will make her famous!' asserted Eugène Blocque.

'Being in my painting will make her even more famous!' asserted Gaston Tacquelle, before both painters collapsed in a mutual bout of coughing.

'And the young *mademoiselle*'s looks,' observed a passing waiter, 'are very close to the Platonic form, as individuated in his Socratic dialogues, of ideal beauty.'

It was a long time since Dimpsy Wickett-Coote had had such a good evening.

*   *   *

Twinks sipped champagne in their suite at the Hôtel de Crillon. Neither she nor her brother were any the worse for their adventures in Notre-Dame, but both of them felt an angry sense of failure. To have been so close to retrieving the stolen Ruperts and then to lose them . . . it was enough to get anyone vinegared off.

'What are we going to do then, Twinks me old toothbrush?' asked Blotto.

'Well, Blotto me old sock-suspender, let's just assess how much new information we've got.'

'I didn't know we'd got any,' said Blotto.

'Oh yes we have, we've got jeroboamsful of the stuff.' Her brother waited patiently, his brain in its customary state of vacancy waiting to be filled. 'For a start we now know for certain that the Vicomte and Vicomtesse de Sales-Malincourt—or the Maharajah and Rani of Pranjipur—or whoever they really were—were not working alone.'

'How do we know that, Twinks me old trouser turn-up?'

'Because they were coffinated. They'd served their master's purpose and he had no further use for them. Also, given that they're both now plum jam on the floor of Notre-Dame, we know they weren't the ones who took the paintings away in the hot-air balloon.'

'So who do you think that was?'

'I'd bet a guinea to a groat that they were *les rats de Paris*.'

'Ah, now I've heard of those boddos.' Slowly the recollection returned to him. 'Yes, someone told me about them.'

'Who?'

Blotto suddenly—and for no reason that he could properly explain—felt embarrassed about mentioning Fifi. 'Oh, just some old chap I met,' he mumbled.

'And I believe,' said Twinks, 'that *les rats de Paris* are in the pay of someone called La Puce.'

'Yes, she said that too.'

His sister didn't pick up on the inconsistency of

129

his informant's gender, but asked where he'd been when he'd heard *les rats de Paris* mentioned.

So Blotto gave her a quick résumé of his evening with Corky Froggett (who was at that moment sleeping off his concussion in his lodgings). The top hat was produced and the two bullet holes in it duly pointed out.

'But they nearly killed you, Blotto!'

'Suppose they did, me old carpet bag.' He'd rather forgotten that in the evening's subsequent excitements. He then filled his sister in on what had happened as he left the Folies Bergère.

'So you actually saw *les rats de Paris*?'

'Certainly did. Did you?'

'No. There wasn't a sight line from that niche in Notre-Dame. But I'd put my last shred of laddered silk stocking on the fact that they sabotaged that trapdoor. And that they were the ones who took away the Ruperts in the hot-air balloon. Hm, and you say they were very small, Blotters.'

'Yes, midgets really.'

'And there were more than two of them?'

'I only saw two, but Fi— my informant said there were lots of them here in Paris.'

'And all in the pay of La Puce . . .' Twinks tapped a contemplative finger on the point of her perfect chin. 'We need to find out more about La Puce, don't we?'

'You're bong on the nose there. How do we do that?'

A smile irradiated his sister's countenance. 'We do what we always do when we're stuck in a swamphole without a tow-rope.' She reached across to the telephone and removed the mouthpiece from its stand. 'We consult Professor

Erasmus Holofernes.'

It took all of Twinks's considerable feminine charms to persuade the night porter at St Raphael's College, Oxford, that the Professor would not mind being woken up to talk to her. The don was, the porter explained, very particular about getting his nine hours' sleep, an essential part of the maintenance routine for his gigantic brain. When, some years before, he'd been woken by a college servant because the room below his was on fire, Professor Holofernes had done his utmost to have the man sacked. It would be more than the porter's job was worth to . . .

But Twinks prevailed, as she always did. The Professor may have vented his fury on the unfortunate porter, but by the time he was through to his caller, he couldn't have been more charming or more delighted to hear from her.

'What is it, my dear? What can I do for you?'

'I'm in Paris, Razzy. Need some dope on a filth-fingering stencher called La Puce.'

'Ah.'

Something in the Professor's voice made her ask, 'You've heard of him?'

'A little. Give me half an hour and I'll telephone you back with more.'

Twinks replaced the receiver and smiled serenely at her brother. 'Soon we'll know everything there is to know,' she announced.

Her mind's eye pictured the scene at St Raphael's College. Though Professor Erasmus Holofernes's room resembled nothing so much as a paper store that had been in the path of a hurricane, his mental filing system could find any document he needed within seconds. His extensive

131

international correspondence brought sackloads of mail to the porter's lodge every morning. Professor Erasmus Holofernes did basically know everything about everything.

Blotto and Twinks's mood had mellowed. Their tantalizing failure to rescue the Ruperts earlier that evening seemed less important now Razzy was on the case. They sipped their champagne in companionable silence.

It was exactly twenty-eight minutes later that the phone rang. Twinks snatched it up. 'What's the bizz-buzz, Razzy?'

'My advice to you, young lady,' came the reply, 'is to be extremely careful in any investigations you make into the activities of the one who is known as La Puce. You are dealing with a very dangerous individual.'

'Larksissimo!' said Twinks.

'He heads a large criminal organization whose tentacles spread into most European countries. He controls this empire through a network of spies, thieves and murderers. These acolytes have different names in the different countries. In France they are known as . . .'

He left a dramatic pause, into which Twinks leapt with the words, '*Les rats de Paris.*'

'Exactly so. And he always recruits midgets. This is because in many cities La Puce uses the sewers as thoroughfares for his criminal activity, and the midgets can run through spaces and tunnels that would be difficult for men of normal size.'

'Is La Puce himself also a midget?' asked Twinks.

From the other end of the line Professor Erasmus Holofernes tutted with annoyance. 'This is a question to which I am afraid I cannot provide

132

an answer. Though much is known about the crimes committed by La Puce, virtually nothing is known about the man himself. It is believed that he operates under the cover of someone whose business affairs are completely above-board. Someone who can infiltrate himself into high society without raising suspicion. Who that person is, though, nobody knows.'

'But do you have any idea where we might find him?'

'On that matter I have some information, but sadly not very much. The crimes of La Puce are very distinctive. They bear, as it were, his *imprimatur*. And from the concentration of such crimes in a certain area it has over the years been possible to deduce where he is operating. Twelve years ago the concentration was in Vienna. Then Oslo, Frankfurt, Genoa and Seville. In recent months the concentration of his characteristic crimes has been on the French Riviera.'

'Then,' announced Twinks, with a wink to her brother, 'it is to the French Riviera that we will go!'

17

To the Riviera!

It was with some relief that Dimpsy Wickett-Coote received the message that had been rung through to Les Deux Mangetouts. Her best friend Twinks would be leaving Paris the following morning on her way to the South of France. The problem of competition for Dimpsy had suddenly disappeared.

So it was with a broad smile that she passed on the news to the group sipping their illegal *absinthe* around the table.

The Marquis of Bluntleigh immediately rose to his feet. 'I must follow Twinks to the Riviera,' he announced, and left the café.

That didn't worry Dimpsy too much. The Marquis had never made any kind of play for her, so his absence would not present any problems. So long as she'd got four men drooling over her, Dimpsy Wickett-Coote was quite content.

But then Eugène Blocque rose to his feet and announced, 'I too must follow Twinks to the Riviera,' before leaving.

Not to be outdone, Gaston Tacquelle, using exactly the same words, followed him out.

Dimpsy turned up the wattage of her best smile and focused it on the two American writers.

'Holy cow,' said Chuck Waggen, rising to his feet. 'I gotta go. Follow Twinks. To the Riviera.'

Of course Scott Frea couldn't allow his rival unimpeded access to the girl in the South of France, so he leapt up and announced his intentions of following Twinks to the Riviera.

The smile froze on Dimpsy's face. The waiter who came forward to collect the *absinthe* glasses tried to cheer her. 'It is for such moments of accidie that one should turn to Boethius's *Consolations of Philosophy*, for its evaluation of the internalized virtues in a—'

'Stuff a pillow in it!' said Dimpsy Wickett-Coote, as she stormed out of Les Deux Mangetouts.

                    *   *   *

Corky Froggett insisted that he was fine to drive. 'If we'd been slowed down by little things like concussion or fatal wounds we wouldn't have given Jerry the pasting we did in the last dust-up,' he assured his master.

But Blotto thought it would still be safer if he took the wheel. Besides, he rather relished the prospect of opening up the Lagonda's throttle on the empty roads of France. The further they left Paris behind, the warmer the weather became and after a couple of hours' driving they put the roof down. Their leather helmets and goggles protected them from the worst of the cold, and the air that rushed past them was bracing.

The roads were slow and frequently rural, so they broke their journey at a small hotel. Blotto didn't think much of the *menu gastronomique* that was offered. Why did the French always have to spoil perfectly good ingredients by smothering them with sauces? And carefully picking out every last clove of garlic still didn't remove the taste of the stuff from his food. However, they all slept well and, though Blotto couldn't understand the hotel's inability to rustle up something as simple as bacon and eggs, they set off the next morning in good spirits.

Blotto had been to the South of France before, with some Old Etonian chums a few years after they left the school, but he hadn't seen much except for the inside of casinos and the bottom of champagne bottles. Still, even though every mile he drove took him further away from his beloved

Tawcester Towers, the prospect of the Riviera was more appealing than that of Paris. At least, so far as he knew, there weren't any art galleries on the Riviera.

18

A Friend in the Right Place

One of the many advantages of being a member of the English aristocracy is that wherever you go in Europe you're bound to have some kind of relative there. The time-honoured custom of treating marriage as a form of trade (though of course never marrying anyone *from* trade) had led to much inbreeding among noble families. And though individual aristocrats might suffer from the excesses of revolution, war or communism, people like Blotto and Twinks could almost always count on finding some distantly connected scion of the family tree wherever their travels took them. They had distant cousins everywhere.

The relevant relative on the Riviera was the Honourable Giles Strappe-Cash. He wasn't from a part of the Lyminster dynasty that one would particularly brag about. In fact there were rumours that among his ancestors was one of the many bastard children of Rupert the Libertine. And that that ancestor's mother had been a particularly juicy washerwoman.

Nor was Giles one of the wealthy members of the Lyminster family. Born from a line of younger sons, his ancestors' prospects had been further reduced over the years by the usual depredations of maintaining country houses, investing in demonstrably stupid business schemes, having expensive mistresses and losing money at cards. As a result, Giles Strappe-Cash was born in debt, and throughout his life had continued to make that debt larger. Expelled from Eton for dubious practices behind the cricket pavilion, he became an enduring source of embarrassment and scandal to the Lyminster family. So much so that he was eventually packed off to the South of France with a small allowance, completely inadequate to the kind of lifestyle he regarded as his birthright.

Having been turned out of decreasingly grand hotels all along the Riviera for non-payment of bills, the Honourable Giles Strappe-Cash had ended up by the time of Blotto and Twinks's arrival in cheap lodgings in the dingy fishing village of Saint-Tropez. There he continued to enjoy his dubious practices, all the while bouncing cheques with the abandon of a small child with a rubber ball.

Twinks had contacted him from Paris and he'd agreed to meet them in a small establishment called the Café Floure in Saint-Tropez. When they arrived there, Corky Froggett—now fully recovered from his concussion—went off in the Lagonda to check their luggage into the recently opened Hôtel Majestic in Cannes.

It was actually mild enough to sit outside the café, and that was where they found their distant cousin. Giles was wearing a battered straw hat and a stained white suit. From his lower lip, above where most people would have a chin (he was from the unchinned side of the Lyminster family) depended a foul-smelling Gauloise cigarette. In front of him on the zinc table was a glass and a half-full bottle of brandy. His manner—and his breath—suggested that he had already ingested the other half.

The Café Floure did not have quite the stature and ambience of Les Deux Mangetouts in Paris. The waiter who took their orders gave only the briefest of disquisitions on Hegelian Dialectic before going off to fetch their coffee.

'Hello,' said Giles Strappe-Cash when Blotto and Twinks had introduced themselves. 'Can you lend me a fiver?'

'Tickey-tockey,' said Blotto, handing across a crisp white note.

The speed with which it was pocketed made the movement almost indiscernible to the human eye. 'Actually, could you make it two?' asked Giles.

'Good ticket,' said Blotto, handing across another.

'And while you're at it, three would—'

Twinks interrupted before her brother could hand over the third note. 'Giles, we're here because we're on the track of two paintings that were stolen from Tawcester Towers.'

'Oh well, you've called in at the wrong shop, I'm afraid. I've never stolen any paintings.' The idea seemed to intrigue him. 'Though, actually, it's something I might have a go at. I pongle off to lots of stately piles and I'm sure the owners wouldn't notice the odd missing portrait of—'

'No, no, Giles. I wasn't suggesting that you yourself were the filth-fingered filcher. But I thought, with your contacts here on the Riviera, you might be able to point our canoes in the right direction.'

'Oh, I read your semaphore. You want to pay me as an agent to introduce you to some of the right people?'

'We weren't actually thinking of paying you.'

'Pity.'

'Though I suppose we could,' said Blotto.

Giles Strappe-Cash leapt on this moment of weakness. 'Elegant idea. So you may as well give me that third fiver to get my brain-juices going.'

'Beezer notion,' said Blotto, handing the note across.

It was pocketed as imperceptibly as its predecessors. 'Right, Twinks, the fact that you've come all the way down here must mean that you have an idea who's behind the theft of the paintings.'

'Yes, we believe the boddo's a criminal mastermind called La Puce.'

Giles nodded in recognition and took a long swallow of brandy. 'There are a lot of people down here looking for La Puce.'

'Including, presumably, the local *gendarmerie*?'

Their distant cousin shook his head. 'They don't seem too aerated about catching him. General view on the Riviera is that La Puce has paid off the police chief. Among other people.'

'And no one knows where to find him?'

'If they do, they're not sharing the information. Another general view on the Riviera is La Puce has got a front.'

'Surely everyone's got a front,' said Blotto. 'And a back.'

'No, I mean that he's got a respectable front. He's a recognized member of Riviera society with a criminal *alter ego*.'

'Ah.' Blotto looked blank. He'd never been much good at Latin.

'If that's the case, Giles,' said Twinks, 'any ideas where we should start looking?'

'Well, you need to make contact with a boddo who knows everyone down here.'

'And is that person you?'

'Sadly no. I used to know quite a lot of Riviera people, but . . .' he cleared his throat and took another swig of brandy, 'a lot of them don't talk to me any more.'

'Why's that?' asked Blotto, unaware of the message in Twinks's face firmly saying that he shouldn't.

'Oh, anti-British prejudice, I think,' replied Giles Strappe-Cash airily. 'And a few misunderstandings about . . . I don't know. People round here do have some rather old-fashioned views about the payment of bills.'

'So who can you recommend down here who does know everyone?' asked Twinks with some urgency.

'Ah, well, there's only one person who fits that pigeonhole. Westmoreland Hubely.'

'The writer?'

'You're bong on the nose there, Twinks. Yes, expatriate Englishman, hugely successful, loaded down with spondulicks. Lives in a huge pile called the Villa Marzipan over Monaco way. Now Westmoreland Hubely really does know everybody.'

'And can you organize an introduction to him for us?'

'Of course I can, Twinks.'

'Larksissimo!'

'Hoopee-doopee!'

'Oh, by the way, Blotto,' asked Giles Strappe-Cash, 'you couldn't see your way to lending me a fiver, could you?'

'Tickey-tockey.' And another note was handed across.

19

The Villa Marzipan

Westmoreland Hubely had the face of an elderly turtle that had just found something it didn't like on the seabed. He welcomed his aristocratic guests to the Villa Marzipan for lunch the next day. Giles Strappe-Cash, who had effected the introduction by telephone, had not been invited. The writer explained, 'I'm afraid he is *persona non grata* here,' making Blotto once again wish he'd paid more attention in Latin lessons.

Blotto had spent the previous evening in a casino with Giles, losing large amounts of money, both from his own bad luck and from the subs he kept giving his distant cousin. Twinks had spent the time interrogating fellow guests at the Hôtel Majestic about the identity of La Puce. She had had no success, though inevitably all of the young men she questioned had fallen in love with her. If you were Twinks, that was just an occupational hazard.

The Villa Marzipan dominated a splendid location looking out over the Mediterranean. Even in early December no one needed topcoats. Westmoreland Hubely's hospitality was legendary. He always had a large number of houseguests from whom he shut himself off in the mornings while he did his writing. But that day most of his visitors had gone out to the casinos of Cannes and the only other guest was a very beautiful dark-haired American girl. She wore a black dress with white trimmings and her eyes were rimmed with kohl make-up. Their host introduced her as 'Mimsy La Pim, the film star'.

'Pleased to meet you, I'm sure,' she squeaked in the voice of a five-year-old. In spite of her looks, she didn't seem one of those actresses likely to make the transition from silent movies to talkies.

'Are you really "Honourables"?' she asked. 'I mean, aristocrats?'

'We are the son and daughter of a duke,' replied Twinks.

'Gee, I never thought I'd meet a real aristocrat. We don't have aristocrats in America. Or a Royal Family. We have a lot of cattle, though. And hot dogs.'

'And what are you doing in France?' asked Twinks. 'Are you making a film?'

'Gee, no. We don't make films here. We make films in Hollywood. No, I'm here to explore my family history.' She fluttered her long dark eyelashes. '"La Pim" is a French word. "La" means "the" in French, and "Pim" means . . . well, "Pim", I guess.'

'And what is a "Pim"?' asked Blotto.

Mimsy shrugged her elegant shoulders. 'I don't know. I haven't got that far in my French lessons yet.'

142

Twinks had noticed a strange quality in her brother's voice when he spoke to Mimsy, and she looked across to see if anything was wrong with him. On his face she saw an expression that she had never seen before. His fine jaw hung open. His glazed eyes gazed. He had the bemused look of one of those dead pharaohs whose brain had just been hooked out through his nose prior to mummification. Was it possible that her brother, the Honourable Devereux Lyminster, had finally met a woman who had stirred his torpid libido? Had Blotto succumbed to what in the country where they now were would be described as a *coup de foudre*?

Whatever was happening, it didn't seem to be totally one-sided either. Mimsy La Pim also wore the expression of one who had unwittingly undergone the removal of vital organs. Her plumply cushioned lips hung open, her kohl-circled eyes stared in amazement and her breathing seemed to have accelerated. Had she been in a scene from one of her silent movies, all that would have been required was a tastefully bordered caption bearing the words: 'It was love at first sight.'

Twinks wasn't so impressed by what was happening with Mimsy. She had frequently witnessed young women licking their lips and positively drooling at the sight of her brother. But she'd never seen him show more than a polite passing interest in the adorer. Though, given the personality and priorities of his mother, Blotto recognized that he would be forced to succumb to matrimony at some point, he was in no hurry to name the unhappy day. And when that awful doom

143

was finally unavoidable, it had never occurred to him that the second party in the contract might be anyone who hadn't been chosen for him by the Dowager Duchess. The idea that he should meet and fall in love with a person of the female gender who hadn't been rigorously selected by his mother had never entered his head.

That was, until the moment he first set eyes on Mimsy La Pim . . . or perhaps it should be said: the real Mimsy La Pim. Because Blotto had seen her image many times at the cinematograph. He had a secret addiction to the kind of slushy melodramas in which she featured. He became more moved than he would care to admit by tales of thwarted love, unsympathetic parents, infants swapped in their cradles and moustache-twirling villains tying innocent young girls to railway lines. And he particularly liked flicks that featured Mimsy La Pim. There was something about the mute appeal in her large eyes that brought out the chivalry in him. He wished he could ride up gallantly on his hunter Mephistopheles to release her from the railway line. And bathe in the benison of her gratitude.

But Blotto did know the difference between the movies and real life. Back in England he had recognized that Mimsy La Pim was likely to remain a fantasy love object in his life. He never expected to see her in the flesh. But now that unlikely event had occurred, the groundwork had been done and he was already prepared to feel a lot for her.

He had to admit that she did stir strange feelings within him, wobbly sensations in his stomach, sensations that he couldn't just put down to all

144

those fumacious sauces the French insisted on covering perfectly good food with.

This highly significant coincidence of attraction all took place very quickly, so that there was hardly a second's pause before Westmoreland Hubely added his comment to the discussion of Mimsy's origins. 'I think it's highly unlikely that you will find any family here in France, Miss La Pim.'

'Gee, why's that, Mr Hubely?'

'Because "Mimsy La Pim" is not your real name, is it?'

Bewilderment wrinkled her perfect brow. 'That's what I'm called.'

'Yes, you're called that, but only because a Hollywood publicist decided that "Pookie Klunch" was not an ideal name for a star of the silver screen.'

'Yes, but I'm not Pookie Klunch any more. Nobody calls me that.'

'Not even your parents?' asked Twinks.

'No,' the film star replied. 'The same publicist who changed my name to Mimsy La Pim also decided that my real parents weren't suitable for a star of the silver screen, what with them working in hog-wrangling and all that. So in all the press handouts it says that I come from an aristocratic French family. And it's that family that I'm hoping to meet up with here in France.'

'But,' said Westmoreland Hubely, who was getting near to exasperation, 'you must realize that you have no chance of meeting people who don't exist.'

'We don't know they don't exist,' said Mimsy. 'And I've always felt much more like a Mimsy La Pim than a Pookie Klunch.'

145

'So how would you explain that you were brought up on a farm in Idaho rather than in a French chateau?'

'I was taken from my cot and changed at birth for the daughter of those hog-farmers.'

'But that kind of thing never happens!' protested Westmoreland Hubely.

'It does too. It's happened in the last three movies I've made. So it must be true.'

The writer being too flabbergasted for speech, Blotto took the opportunity to add chivalrous support to his new love. 'Mimsy's right. You only have to look at her to see that she has innate breeding.'

The film star looked across and smiled gratitude at him. The pair gazed soupily into each other's eyes and in that moment Twinks suddenly understood the secret of the attraction between the two. Her brother had finally met a woman who had exactly the same intellectual capacity as he had. Just as deep calleth unto deep, so vacancy calleth unto vacancy.

Anyway, Twinks wasn't on the Riviera to worry about her brother's love life. Their trip had a more important purpose. So turning the sparkling azure beam of her eyes on to Westmoreland Hubely's hooded ones, she asked, 'Do you know anything about the criminal mastermind called La Puce?'

The writer was far too canny an old bird to make elaborate shows of emotion, but a slight tic on his upper right-hand cheek showed that the question had relevance for him. Rather than answering, however, he just announced, 'I think the weather is clement enough for us to take our cocktails outside.'

146

He was right. The sides of the terrace at the Villa Marzipan were shielded by glass screens and, with no wind to dilute it, the winter sun was surprisingly warm. An attractive houseboy of oriental origin brought out a tray with an array of most of the world's liquors on it and asked which cocktails the writer's guests would favour.

Blotto's customary tipples were vintage wines and brandies, but he did recall the beneficial effects of something called a St Louis Steamhammer which had been mixed for him by a barman at the Savoy. Without much expectation that the houseboy would have heard of it, he said that's what he'd like, and was gratified to have it immediately created for him.

Mimsy La Pim, though obviously asked before him, delayed ordering until she had seen what Blotto was opting for and then said she'd have the same. Twinks chose a Cobbler's Awl, and Westmoreland Hubely asked for 'My usual Martini, dry as a Muslim Christmas'.

They were soon joined for cocktails by a youngish man introduced by the writer as 'Derek Gringe, my secretary'. Blotto couldn't help observing that the newcomer's accent and manners definitely marked him out as from the oikish classes. He also thought that Westmoreland Hubely and Derek Gringe's conversation contained more whispering and giggling than he would have expected from a normal master/secretary relationship. Still, the writer hadn't got any real breeding, only vast amounts of money, so perhaps his closeness to someone only a couple of rungs down the social ladder was not so remarkable, after all.

Blotto noticed that his sister kept trying to get back on to the subject of La Puce, but each time she raised it, Westmoreland Hubely managed gracefully to steer the conversation round to other topics. Most of which were indiscreet anecdotes about the various crowned heads and luminaries of the arts world who had been his previous houseguests. Twinks conjectured which of their own Lyminster family quirks and oddities would provide gossip-fodder to be sniggered over with Derek Gringe after they had departed the Villa Marzipan.

Blotto didn't think anything of the sort. Conjecture had never been his strong suit. He just shared soupy looks with Mimsy La Pim, while the St Louis Steamhammers quietly fricasséed their brains.

From Westmoreland Hubely's behaviour Twinks deduced that he knew a lot more about the identity of La Puce than he was prepared to divulge.

20

A Top-Secret Conversation

After a second round of cocktails another oriental houseboy, at least as beautiful as the first, came out on to the terrace to announce that luncheon was served. Derek Gringe led the ladies into the house, but Westmoreland Hubely, after peremptorily dismissing the two houseboys, said to Blotto, 'Wait a moment. There's something important I want to talk to you about, Devereux.'

'Please call me Blotto. Everyone does,' said Blotto. He was rather excited at being detained in this way. Granted, it would deprive him for a few moments of the sight of Mimsy La Pim, but that minus had to be measured against the great plus of getting closer to the stolen Ruperts. Maybe, Blotto reasoned, Westmoreland Hubely, assuming (incorrectly) the male to be the senior partner in the siblings' investigative team, was intending to share with him what he knew about La Puce. That'd be pure creamy éclair. Blotto always relished the idea of passing on to his sister vital information that he'd found out off his own bat. It was rarely that he could get one over on Twinks. He might even find himself employing that childhood expression of oneupmanship: 'So snubbins to you, Twinks!'

He thought it was promising that Westmoreland Hubely asked him to sit down on a lounging sofa and also that the writer sat so close to him, suggesting that the information about to be imparted was top-secret stuff.

'There's something I want to tell you,' whispered the older man.

This too was promising. 'Well, come on, uncage the ferrets,' said Blotto.

'You're one of the most attractive young men I've ever seen.'

'Oh, don't talk such toffee.'

'You know,' Westmoreland Hubely whispered on, 'a lot of us go through life pretending to be

149

something we're not, hiding our real identity under some mask of convention.' So caught up was he in what he was saying, the writer had unwittingly placed his hand on Blotto's knee as he asked, 'You do know what I'm talking about, don't you, Blotto?'

'Oh yes. I read your semaphore.'

'Good.' For some reason the writer's hand was now stroking Blotto's knee.

'What you're talking about, Mr Hubely, is La Puce.'

'What?'

'You're telling me how La Puce hides his real identity under a mask of convention.'

'No, no. Are you being deliberately obtuse?'

Blotto denied the accusation. He'd never in his life encountered the necessity of being *deliberately* obtuse.

'Let me approach this from another angle,' said Westmoreland Hubely. 'You went to English public school, didn't you?'

'Tickey-tockey.'

'Then you must know what I'm talking about. When you were in your dorm . . .'

'Didn't have dorms at Eton.'

'All right. When you were in the changing rooms after games, you must have known that some of the boys got up to things which . . . well, were regarded as illegal.'

'Ah.' Understanding dawned on Blotto. 'On the same page with you now.'

'You understand what I'm saying?'

'Yes, I do, by Denzil!'

'Good.' Westmoreland Hubely's unconscious stroking of Blotto's thigh had become more

150

vigorous.

'Yes.' Blotto nodded. 'You're saying that La Puce went to Eton. Bit outside the rule-book, that. I mean, one liked to think the kind of boddos one shared muffins with at Eton were—'

'No, no, no!' the writer cried in exasperation. 'What I'm saying is that there's a side of your nature that you've never admitted to, a side which perhaps you don't think exists, but which I can see is blatantly there in your personality.'

'Ah.' Blotto was silent for a moment. Then he said, 'I think I'm on the same page with you now, Mr Hubely.'

'Good. And what I'm saying is that the right person . . . let's say me . . . could awaken that side of your personality . . . and you would feel much better, much less frustrated, if I were to awaken it.'

'Do you really think you could?' asked Blotto eagerly.

'I'm sure I could,' breathed Westmoreland Hubely, whose hand was still thigh-stroking, while his other arm had somehow got itself round the younger man's neck. So, Blotto realized, what they were talking about really was top-secret stuff.

'That'd really be the lark's larynx!' said Blotto excitedly.

'So are you ready to have that other side of your nature unlocked?'

'I certainly am. I always rather suspected that I did have this other side of my nature, you know. Others of my muffin-toasters at Eton seemed to accept it without donning their worry-boots, but for me it was always a tough rusk to chew. So how exactly are you going to do the unlocking? What is it I have to do?'

'You have to come to a party that I'm giving here at Villa Marzipan this evening. And you have to come ready to abandon all your inhibitions, prepared for anything.'

'Good ticket!'

'And I can promise you an encounter that will change your whole outlook on life.'

'Hoopee-doopee!'

Westmoreland Hubely removed his hand and arm from Blotto's anatomy and said wryly, 'Fulfilment is always the sweeter for being deferred.'

Blotto reckoned another 'Hoopee-doopee!' was probably the best response to that.

'And now,' said the writer, 'let's join the ladies—in which category of course . . .' he sniggered, 'I also include Derek.'

Blotto hadn't a mouse-squeak of an idea what that meant, but he knew for certain that it was lunchtime. And that he was spoffingly hungry.

*　　*　　*

The meal was a bit of a strain for Blotto. Not that the food wasn't excellent, and impeccably served by more beautiful oriental houseboys. It was just that he was desperate to tell Twinks about his conversation with Westmoreland Hubely, and he couldn't do that until they were alone.

So while the writer and his secretary continued to shred the reputations of actors, actresses, kings and queens (particularly queens), Blotto had to contain his excitement. The only compensation was that, seated opposite Mimsy La Pim, he was able to spend the entire meal gazing at his new

152

object of adoration.

They didn't talk much. They didn't need to. The bond they had instantly formed was too deep for words. But at one point, in a lull in the general conversation, Blotto did observe, 'You know, Mimsy, I'm really surprised to see your lips are red.'

'Gee, why's that?'

'Because in every film of yours I've seen they've been black.'

'Yes, that's funny,' she said, 'I've noticed that too. And yet when I look at myself in the mirror before filming—and after filming—they're definitely red.'

'That's a rum baba,' said Blotto. 'Do you have any explanation for why it happens?'

'Well,' said Mimsy La Pim, 'I've thought about it and I have got an explanation for it. You know how in the dark things look dark?'

'Tickey-tockey.'

'Well, the only times I've ever been in a cinematograph to see a movie, all the lights have been turned off.'

'I've noticed that too,' Blotto agreed.

'So it's no surprise that everything looks dark. And that's why my lips look black. If they showed the films with the lights on, my lips'd look red.'

'Toad-in-the-hole . . .' Blotto was impressed by her logic and reasoning. What a wonderful piece of womanflesh! Not only was Mimsy La Pim a paragon of pulchritude, he now knew that she was highly intelligent too.

*   *   *

It was not until they were in the Lagonda with

153

Corky Froggett driving them away from the Villa Marzipan that Blotto got a chance to tell Twinks his great news.

'We've finally got some good guff on La Puce!'

'Have we? Where from?'

'Westmoreland Hubely. He told me on the terrace after you and Mimsy had gone in to lunch.'

His sister couldn't help asking, 'Why did he tell you?'

Blotto coughed modestly. 'I think he made the assumption that I was the brains in our investigative team.'

A choice of reactions to this assertion came into Twinks's mind, but she had too generous a spirit to voice any of them.

'What's more,' Blotto went on excitedly, 'soon I'm going to be brainier still!'

'Oh?'

'Yes, Westmoreland Hubely said that I'd got another side of my nature that had never been properly expressed, but that he could unlock it.'

'Really?'

'Yes. Isn't that exciting?'

'Well, I'm not entirely sure that—'

'Don't you see? What he could recognize—and what nobody else has ever recognized, least of all the beaks at Eton—is that I have a very powerful intellect. That's what he was saying. And that's what he's proposing to unlock!'

'Are you sure that's what he meant?' asked his sister dubiously.

'As sure as the odds-on favourite in a one-horse race, Twinks me old cabbage patch. He meant that, once it was unlocked, my intellect would be way up there on a level with yours. Which was

154

why,' Blotto added modestly, 'he passed on the information about La Puce to me rather than to you.'

'Oh yes, La Puce. What did he say about the stencher?'

'Westmoreland Hubely told me a couple of very interesting things about that particular lump of toadspawn. First—and this was a big surprise to me—the stencher went to Eton! Well, you could have knocked me down with a piece of tissue paper when I heard that. And second, La Puce will actually be at a party that Hubely's giving at the Villa Marzipan this very evening!'

'Are you sure?'

'As sure as a lawyer's bill arriving by return of post, Twinks me old backscratcher. And Hubely's going to introduce La Puce to me! Yes, he promised me "an encounter that will change my whole outlook on life"!'

Once again Twinks found herself asking, 'Are you sure that's what he meant, Blotters?'

21

A Marvellous Party

There was a bit of a stye in the eye for Blotto when they got back to the Hôtel Majestic. Corky Froggett had seen to it that their luggage had been taken up to their suite, where it had been unpacked by the valet and housemaid appointed to them by the management. But when Blotto was going through his things, preparatory to dressing for Westmoreland Hubely's party, he could find no sign of his precious cricket bat.

His first thought was to blame the valet, but an extensive interview with the hotel's manager seemed to prove that no guilt could be attributed there. The valet, when summoned, clearly wouldn't have recognized what a cricket bat was, let alone imagined that a battered piece of willow would have had any value.

Blotto checked with Corky Froggett, who had no recollection of having seen the bat when he packed the bags into the Lagonda in Paris. So perhaps it had been stolen from the Hôtel de Crillon.

Whatever had happened to it, the bat's absence put a bit of a candle-snuffer on Blotto's habitually cheery world-view. If they were up against the kind of stenchers who stole cricket bats, he and Twinks were going to have their work cut out on the Riviera.

The theft was a bad omen, and Blotto approached the evening that lay ahead with a degree of foreboding.

*   *   *

It was clearly true that Westmoreland Hubely did know *everyone*. Had the newspapers' gossip columns contrived to infiltrate a photographer into the Villa Marzipan that evening, they would have stocked up with a decadesworth of scandal and tittle-tattle. Princesses misbehaved noisily with silent film stars. Princes and politicians compromised each other. Popular singers fraternized with archbishops. Ex-kings rubbed shoulders (among other things) with x-rated courtesans.

Alcohol, drugs and other services were generously supplied by beautiful oriental houseboys. There was a jazz band for those who wished to dance and an apparently infinite number of bedrooms for those who wanted to put their feet up (among other things).

But all Blotto wanted to do was to have his meeting with La Puce, recover the Gainsborough and Reynolds and get back to Tawcester Towers for Christmas.

Nor did he plan to return home alone. As well as Twinks and Corky Froggett, there was a third person he planned to have with him in the Lagonda. As soon as he'd arrived at Villa Marzipan he had sought out Mimsy La Pim. He found her on the sheltered terrace looking out at the lights of fishing boats bobbing about on the Mediterranean. She sat beside a table on which was a cheeseboard dominated by a full circle of Brie, from which she cut occasional segments.

Having found the object of his affections, Blotto then proceeded to have a very serious conversation with her. It went like this:

BLOTTO: Good evening.
MIMSY: Good evening.
BLOTTO: I see you're still here.
MIMSY: Yes, I'm still here.
BLOTTO: Tickey-tockey. Because if you weren't still here, I wouldn't be talking to you, would I?
MIMSY: I guess not.
A silence ensued while they gazed soupily at each other.

157

MIMSY: There's one thing I wanted to
   ask you, Blotto. . .
BLOTTO: Ask away, me old fruitbat.
MIMSY: What does your wife do?
BLOTTO: Do?
MIMSY: Yes. Don't you understand the
   word?
BLOTTO: Yes. But not when it's applied to
   women in my class. They don't do anything.
MIMSY: So your wife doesn't have a job?
BLOTTO: Toad-in-the-hole, no. No wife of
   mine would ever have a job. That'd be totally
   beyond the barbed wire.
MIMSY [*disappointed*]:   So where is your wife
   now?
BLOTTO: Nowhere.
MIMSY: How does she manage that?
BLOTTO: I don't have a wife.
MIMSY [*gratified*]: Oh, gee. . .
More soupy silence.
BLOTTO: I suppose at some point you'll
   have to pongle back to the old US of A?
MIMSY: Yes, I start making a new picture
   in March.
BLOTTO: Toad-in-the-hole . . . I didn't
   know you were a painter too.
MIMSY: No, no. I don't mean paint a
   picture. I mean act in a picture.
BLOTTO: Ah, read your semaphore.
   Stenchers tying you to railway lines and all
   that rombooley?
MIMSY: I guess so.
BLOTTO: It always puts lumps in my
   custard when I see those fumacious oiks
   doing that to you. I want to jump up on to the

158

screen and coffinate the running sores.

MIMSY: Oh, gee, Blotto, that's very sweet of you.

BLOTTO: I'll want to coffinate them even more now I've actually clapped me peepers on you.

MIMSY: Oh, gee, Blotto. . .

Another soupy silence. Without breaking eye contact, Mimsy slices off another segment of Brie and puts it in her mouth.

MIMSY: I don't know what this stuff is, but it sure tastes wonderful.

BLOTTO: It's Brie.

MIMSY: Brie?

BLOTTO: It's a cheese.

MIMSY: You're joking me. This isn't cheese.

BLOTTO: It is.

MIMSY: No, it isn't. Cheese is yellow and solid like soap. At least it is where I come from.

BLOTTO: I promise you that Brie is cheese.

MIMSY: It can't be. It tastes of something.

Blotto decides not to pursue this line of conversation. An even soupier silence ensues.

BLOTTO: Still, March is more than two months away.

MIMSY: March?

BLOTTO: The month.

MIMSY: Oh.

BLOTTO: It's more than two months away.

MIMSY: Is it?

BLOTTO: Yes, it's December now. Then you've got January and February before you get to March.

159

MIMSY: Have you?

BLOTTO: Yes. [*silence*] You do have the same months in America as we do here?

MIMSY: No.

BLOTTO: Oh?

MIMSY: Well, in America we have January and February. Here they have '*janvier*' and '*fevrier*'.

BLOTTO: Ah, yes. When I said 'here', I meant England. When you're English, 'here' is always England, regardless of wherever you may happen to be.

MIMSY: Ah.

BLOTTO: What about America? Is that 'here' for you?

MIMSY: No, that's in America.

BLOTTO: Wow, you're a bit of a brainbox, aren't you, Mimsy?

MIMSY: Oh, shucks.

Further soupiness.

BLOTTO: Have you ever been to England?

MIMSY: No.

BLOTTO: Would you like to go there?

MIMSY: Sure.

BLOTTO: Good. Well, that's agreed then.

Blotto was relieved at how easy it had all been. He felt sure he hadn't needed to spell out all the details to her. Mimsy La Pim was going to come back with him to Tawcester Towers. There he could introduce her to Mephistopheles and to his collection of cricket bats. And, of course, to the Dowager Duchess. Blotto tried not to let his mind dwell on that particular hazard ahead.

Mimsy La Pim then got swept away from Blotto

by a raucous group of Hollywood types. He was tempted to follow, but decided he didn't need to. They'd had their important conversation and he could catch up with her later. Arranging to meet her back on the terrace in an hour's time, he pongled off to look for Twinks.

She was to be found, inevitably, sitting at a table surrounded by amorous swains. What's more, they were amorous swains Blotto recognized. Blocque and Tacquelle had recently arrived from Paris. So had Chuck Waggen and Scott Frea. And, looking as lugubriously lovelorn as ever, the Marquis of Bluntleigh was also of the party.

(The one member of their Paris entourage who wasn't there was Dimpsy Wickett-Coote. Her nose had been put out of joint while Twinks had been around, but with her best friend absent she was resetting it by taking on industrial quantities of lovers. And her self-esteem, always pretty robust, was once again blossoming. Dimpsy decided that, much as she adored her best friend, their relationship might in future be more satisfactorily conducted by correspondence.)

At the Villa Marzipan Twinks caught her brother's eye as he approached her group of admirers and she mouthed an interrogative 'La Puce?' Blotto shook his head. He had not yet seen Westmoreland Hubely that evening, so the encounter he was so looking forward to had to be postponed. Instead, he had to kill time by listening to the squabbles of his sister's admirers.

'But I cannot continue to paint you down here in the Midi,' Eugène Blocque was protesting. 'The light is totally different. For me to complete the *chef d'oeuvre* of *Triangulisme*, it will be necessary for you to accompany me back to Paris, where I can—'

He was interrupted by a bout of coughing, which gave his rival Gaston Tacquelle the opportunity to chip in. 'You will not have this problem with me, *ma belle* Twinks. The genius of my painting is above such petty considerations as light. All I need to produce the *chef d'oeuvre* of *Triangulisme* is your naked body in front of me and—'

He too succumbed to the coughing, but the two painters' competitive demonstration of the *phtisie* was interrupted by the insinuating voice of Derek Gringe. 'Nasty tickles you've got there. I could introduce you to a very good doctor down here, English fellow called Dr Cooper. He's very good on coughs—sorted out Westmoreland's chest with no problems at all. Would you like me to give you his number?'

Both painters declined the offer. Through their spluttering they managed to assert that their *phtisie* was far too advanced for mere doctors to do anything for them. However good this Dr Cooper might be with chests, he would never have seen cases as serious as theirs. Then they resumed their coughing contest.

This opened up the field for Chuck Waggen and Scott Frea to move in on Twinks. 'What do you say?' asked the muscle-bound Chuck. 'Suppose Scott and I have a drinking contest . . . and you're the prize. The one who's still standing at the end of the evening gets you.'

'You're on,' said Scott Frea before Twinks had an opportunity to respond. 'We're already well oiled,' he announced as he slipped off his chair.

'We've hardly started,' said Chuck Waggen. 'And

I can drink you under the table any day.'

'I already am under the table,' replied Scott's voice from under the table.

'I am sorry that I appear not already to have made it clear,' said Twinks, taking on the intonation of her mother the Dowager Duchess, 'that I am not available to either of you gentlemen—and certainly not as some kind of prize in a drinking contest. I have more important reasons for being down here on the Riviera.'

'Of course,' the Marquis of Bluntleigh agreed. 'But when you have dealt with the business that brought you down here, then maybe you can open your mind to thoughts of love. Do not forget that your mother the Dowager Duchess is very much in favour of our union.' He reached inside his dinner jacket. 'And to show what a Grade A breathsapper I think you are I have written you another poem. In French again.'

Twinks was not so badly brought up as to refuse the tribute, so she took the proffered envelope and placed it in her reticule with vague promises to read it later.

'Did you like the last one?' asked the Marquis.

Neither was Twinks so badly brought up as to admit that she hadn't a bat's squeak of an idea what he was on about and risk crushing what appeared to be Buzzer Bluntleigh's fragile confidence. So she borrowed a trick from her brother's repertoire and just said, 'Hoopee-doopee.'

This seemed to fit the pigeonhole, and the Marquis of Bluntleigh sat back, his hopes still intact. But if he had any illusions about the lack of competition in the Twinks Stakes, these were quickly dispelled.

'I cannot live if you do not come back to Paris, so that I can finish the *chef d'oeuvre* of—' Eugène Blocque began before his words were lost in more coughing.

'Through my painting you will become acknowledged as the most beautiful woman in the—' Coughing also cut off the end of Gaston Tacquelle's sentence.

'Suppose I wrestled a bull for you?' suggested Chuck Waggen. 'Then would you allow me to show my prowess? As a lover.'

'Suppose I . . . wrote a really . . . sensitive book . . . about your tental murmoil?' Scott Frea proposed from under the table.

'I don't have any mental turmoil,' Twinks replied sharply.

'No, but I could . . .' He mumbled on, but nobody listened to him because the party's host had just arrived at their table.

Westmoreland Hubely smiled the leathery smile of a crocodile at Blotto and asked, 'Now, are you ready for that "encounter" we discussed earlier?'

'Tickey-tockey,' said Blotto, and followed the writer towards the staircase of the Villa Marzipan.

*   *   *

The room into which Westmoreland Hubely led Blotto was splendidly appointed, its space dominated by a massive double bed. Though the glass doors to the balcony had been closed, the blinds were not drawn, so they could see the same view of fishing boat lights on the Mediterranean as had been visible from the balcony below.

164

The writer closed the large door to the landing and double-locked it. 'We do not want to be disturbed, do we?'

'No, we don't, by Denzil.' Blotto was impressed by this serious level of security. Clearly what Westmoreland Hubely had to tell him about La Puce was very much inside-of-the-safe stuff.

'Shall we start with a drink?' his host suggested.

'Tickey-tockey by me.'

'Before luncheon you had a St Louis Steamhammer. Would another of those be agreeable?'

'Again tickey-tockey. A sip of one of those spoffers and I feel like my brain's been turned into a hand grenade from which some boddo's just pulled out the pin. After a couple, I have no responsibility for my actions at all.'

'Excellent,' said Westmoreland Hubely in a silky voice, as he poured a large St Louis Steamhammer from a cocktail shaker and handed it across to Blotto. 'I'll go for a brandy. I always find brandy oils the wheels in these situations.'

'Good ticket. I'm all in favour of oiled wheels,' said Blotto.

Westmoreland Hubely sat on the large bed. 'Maybe you'd like to sit beside me?'

Blotto did as instructed and took a long swallow from his glass. There was the customary two-second delay before the firework display detonated inside his head.

'Closer,' said Westmoreland Hubely. Blotto did as instructed. 'Have you been excited since we arranged this encounter, Blotto?'

'I'll say. Couldn't get the old brain on any other track all afternoon.'

'Good.' Once again the writer's hand was on his guest's knee. Bit of a rum baba, thought Blotto. Must be some kind of involuntary tic, like those boddos whose faces keep screwing up. Often caused by shell shock, he'd heard. He wondered whether Westmoreland Hubely had had a nasty basinful during the last little dust-up with Jerry.

Blotto took another draught of St Louis Steamhammer. Jumping crackers started doing a Charleston inside his cranium. 'Anyway, Mr Hubely,' he said, 'you were going to tell me about people hiding their true identity beneath a different exterior . . .'

'I most certainly was.'

'Do you know many people who do that?'

'You'd be surprised how many there are, Blotto.'

'Like who, though? Could you give me a name?'

'Well, the classic example down here on the Riviera would be Derek Gringe.'

Blotto was astounded. 'Derek Gringe your secretary?'

'Of course.'

'I'd never have believed it.'

'Really? Most people who meet him think it's pretty damned obvious.'

'Well, I can't thank you enough, Mr Hubely.' Blotto rose to his feet.

'No, but wait—'

'Sorry, I must go and tell Twinks.'

Blotto turned the two keys in the lock and opened the door to the landing. 'Thanks again,' he cried out as he left. 'You're a Grade A foundation stone, Mr Hubely.'

Rum do, thought Blotto. Why, when he's just done his fellow man such a good deed, was the

166

expression on the writer's face one of disappointment?

*　　*　　*

It took him quite a while to find Twinks amidst the gyrating and intertwined bodies that littered the Villa Marzipan. Which was frustrating, because he was longing to tell her about the huge advance he'd made in their investigation. Off his own bat.

Once he'd finally tracked her down and told her that the mysterious La Puce was none other than Derek Gringe, he was a bit underwhelmed by her reaction.

'Are you sure that's what Westmoreland Hubely meant, Blotters?'

'Of course I am. He couldn't have made it clearer.'

'But I can't see Derek Gringe as an international criminal mastermind.'

'That's the clever thing about it, you see. He hides his true identity under a spoffing front.'

'Hm . . .'

He still didn't get the impression that his sister believed him.

'Shall we go and confront the stencher?'

'No, I'd rather have more proof that he actually is La Puce.'

Blotto had never known Twinks so underwhelmed by a breakthrough in an investigation. But then he reasoned she was probably jealous. It wasn't often that he was the one who cracked a case open. He'd follow up with her later. He knew she'd come round to the idea.

But at that moment a look at his watch told him

he was late for his rendezvous with Mimsy La Pim, so he rushed away. When he had got to the appointed place on the terrace, there was no sign of her. Just the Brie, now reduced to one thin segment.

Blotto kicked himself for being late and spent the rest of the night searching the Villa Marzipan for the beautiful film star. The search involved some moments of deep embarrassment as he opened a variety of bedroom doors.

But by the time streaks of a pinkish dawn were beginning to reflect on the surface of the Mediterranean, Blotto was forced to accept the unpalatable truth.

Mimsy La Pim had vanished.

22

Another Disappearance!

The dawn also brought to Blotto a great doubt as to whether he had correctly identified La Puce. What had seemed so credible in Westmoreland Hubely's bedroom was now decreasingly convincing. There was something about Derek Gringe that ill-suited him to the role of criminal mastermind.

And when Blotto confronted the very hungover secretary the next morning the idea seemed even more remote. The further their conversation developed, the more glad Blotto was that he hadn't actually voiced the accusation. Derek Gringe was creepy, but not evil. Apart from anything else, he had spent the entire previous year at the Villa Marzipan, so he hadn't had much opportunity to organize the dangers that had confronted Blotto and Twinks in Paris.

What's more, he had a very solid alibi for the night of the party. He had apparently spent it in the company of one of the oriental houseboys. Though why, Blotto could not begin to imagine.

Nor could he imagine why Westmoreland Hubely had pointed the finger of suspicion towards his secretary the previous evening. Maybe, thought Blotto, Twinks was right. Maybe I did misunderstand what the writer had been saying. Though if he hadn't been saying that Derek Gringe was La Puce, then what on earth had he been saying? Life was sometimes very confusing if you were Blotto.

All he knew for sure was that Mimsy La Pim had vanished and he was no nearer identifying her abductor.

*   *   *

Blotto was distraught. Twinks had never seen him so distraught. On the rare previous occasions when he had had a night without sleep his first action of the following morning had been to take to his bed and catch up on the beauty stuff. Blotto couldn't really function without his regular eight hours of unconsciousness (and actually he preferred to make it nine . . . or ten). But when they returned to the Hôtel Majestic after the party at the Villa Marzipan, he made no mention of beds or sleep or anything comfortingly soporific.

He just mooned around their suite like a hound

169

who's caught a fox and then had it snatched away from him by other hounds for the tearing-apart climax of the entertainment.

Twinks did her best to cheer him up. 'It's really larksissimo, Blotto me old trombone. It's the next step in our investigation. I'll bet a guinea to a groat that La Puce is behind Mimsy's disappearance. So in a way we've got a new clue, haven't we? And when you rescue her from La Puce, think how grateful she'll be. She won't be able to refuse you anything then.'

'Yes, but suppose we don't manage to rescue her . . .'

'That doesn't sound like you, Blotters. You're usually full of derring-do, not derring-don't. Is this the brother of mine who scored an unbeaten hundred and seventy-six in the Eton and Harrow match? Is this the Blotto who won the Two Hundred Yards Dash with four cracked ribs? You shouldn't let a minor irritant like La Puce put lumps in your custard.'

But her cheering words had about as much effect as a silver candle-snuffer on the Great Fire of London. Blotto's brow remained furrowed.

'Oh, put a jumping cracker under it!' her sister cajoled him. 'Normally the prospect of rescuing a damsel in distress tickles your mustard like a hundred-to-one winner. Remember the larks you had freeing Ex-Princess Ethelinde. Not to mention Laetitia Melmont. Why's Mimsy La Pim different from those two good old greengages?'

Blotto's face sagged with apology and embarrassment as he mumbled, 'Because I really care about her. So far as I'm concerned, Twinks, Mimsy La Pim is absolutely the lark's larynx. I'm

170

going to marry her.'

Twinks's first thought was how the Dowager Duchess would greet the news that her son was planning to marry someone whose real name was Pookie Klunch. And who compounded that social lapse by being American! But she didn't voice her reaction, instead saying, 'Well, surely that's all the more reason why you should shift your shimmy and rescue her.'

'Yes, but suppose I fail? Suppose my attempts to save her put her in further jeopardy?'

'That's just a risk you have to take, Blotters. And, anyway . . .' Twinks broke off and sniffed suspiciously. 'Look, since we've been talking, Blotto, I've been aware of a very strange smell. Have you got a mouse-squeak of an idea what it is?'

'It's probably this.' Blotto removed from his blazer pocket a thin parcel wrapped in greaseproof paper.

The smell that Twinks had mentioned was suddenly stronger. 'Yes, that's certainly it,' she said, clamping thumb and forefinger on to her dainty nose. 'What on earth is it?'

Blotto unwrapped the parcel and looked at its contents with melancholy reverence. 'It's Brie,' he announced. 'The Brie that Mimsy was eating when I last saw her on the terrace of the Villa Marzipan. I will keep it for ever. It may be the only thing of hers that I will ever possess.'

'Of course it won't be, Blotters,' said his sister in the voice she'd used as Captain of Lacrosse at St Wilhelmina's. 'Oh come on, your face is as long as a vicar's sermon. Of course you'll rescue Mimsy. Remember who you are. Remember who we both

171

are. We're Lyminsters, and Lyminsters are never defeated!'

'You're bong on the nose there, Twinks.' The latent fire in Blotto's belly was beginning to rekindle. 'Yes, of course we can rescue Mimsy.'

'That's more like my brave soldier! We can face up to anyone—even La Puce.'

'Yes, it's not the actual facing-up to La Puce that worries me. It's the finding La Puce to face up to.'

'You're right, Blotters. What we need is a really important breakthrough on the case.'

'Do you think you can muster one up, Twinks me old carving fork?'

'I'll do my bounciest to make it work,' she replied.

Blotto was reverently silent. His admiration for his sister was boundless, and he knew that at times she could make a significant advance on an investigation by sheer exercise of willpower. He watched as her azure eyes shut and a fine tracery of lines formed around them with the effort of concentration.

There was a long silence, eventually broken by a tap on the door of their suite. Twinks's brow cleared. 'This'll be it,' she declared. 'The really important breakthrough on the case.'

And so it proved to be. A footman appeared with a letter on a silver salver. It was addressed to 'The Hon. Honoria Lyminster'. The missive had been discovered at the Villa Marzipan and couriered across to the Hôtel Majestic by one of Westmoreland Hubely's oriental houseboys.

As soon as the door had closed behind the footman, Twinks tore the letter open and read:

If you are reading this, then it's a great stroke of luck. I managed to scribble it while I was being abducted from the Villa Marzipan by the villainous acolytes of La Puce. I dropped it, hoping someone would get it to you. La Puce has not only seized me, but also Mimsy La Pim. I don't know where they're taking us, but my mother knows everything that happens on the Riviera. If you were to contact her at the Château d'Erimes, she might be able to send you down in the right direction and all will be well. It's the only hope. With all my love to you, Twinks, and in the (not very strong) hope that we will meet again, Buzzer Bluntleigh.

'What did I say, Blotto me old dose of castor oil?' asked Twinks. 'I think we've got our really important breakthrough on the case.'

23

The Château d'Erimes

The Château d'Erimes perched on a rocky hillside a few miles inland. Despite the distance, it commanded wonderful views of the Mediterranean.

As Corky Froggett brought the Lagonda to a halt at the apex of the semicircular gravel drive, Blotto looked up at the building with distaste. He vaguely remembered from his French lessons at Eton that 'château' meant 'castle', but the place wasn't his idea of a castle. English castles were solid four-square structures built for the serious purpose of repelling the armies of one's foes (or during unfortunate episodes like the Wars of the Roses, one's relations). Whereas the French equivalent was all superfluous detail—lots of turrets with pointed slate roofs. In fact altogether far too many pointed bits. The effect was fussy and over-elaborate. Like their food, thought Blotto.

In the car Twinks had been aware that the smell of the Brie in her brother's pocket was not getting less with the passage of time. She contemplated mentioning it and asking whether Blotto really thought the aroma to be a suitable accompaniment for a social visit. Maybe the proper thing would be to leave the Brie in the Lagonda . . . ? But remembering the reverence with which Blotto had gazed upon this memento of his lost love, she curbed her tongue.

Rather than becoming a dowager, because her son remained as yet unmarried, Buzzer's mother retained her title of the Marchioness of Bluntleigh and it was as such that she introduced herself when Blotto and Twinks were ushered into one of the Château d'Erimes' many drawing rooms.

The Marchioness was all angles, like a stick insect that had recently been on a crash diet. She wore a black lace dress and carried a lorgnette which seemed just to add another spoke to her angularity. Her English was impeccable. Twinks remembered the Marquis of Bluntleigh once telling her that his mother had not been allowed to speak her native tongue in the house of his father, who had tried—quite understandably—to pass his wife off as English.

The social niceties of introduction concluded,

Blotto announced, 'We are here in an attempt to find Buzzer.'

'Buzzer?' the Marchioness echoed in bewilderment.

'Buzzer was the name by which your son was always known at Eton.'

'Why?' asked the old lady. 'I am not aware of my son ever having buzzed.'

'No, no, nicknames aren't given to people for any reason. I mean, our real names are Devereux and Honoria Lyminster, but everyone calls us "Blotto" and "Twinks". The names don't mean anything. That's how it's always worked amongst people of our class in England.'

'Of course I knew that,' the Marchioness said hastily, afraid that her incomprehension might be thought to demonstrate that she was unfamiliar with English customs and possibly even reveal that she was French. Then a new thought came to her. 'Lady Honoria Lyminster . . .' She pronounced the words slowly.

'Yes,' said Twinks, slightly bewildered. 'That's who I said I am.'

'Of course. I know all about you. You are the young woman to whom my son has been paying court back in England.'

'Yes. If "paying court" is how you wish to refer to it.'

The lorgnette was raised to the old lady's eyes for a closer scrutiny. 'Well, you're certainly pretty enough for him to marry. Would you mind standing up for a moment?' Twinks did as she was told. 'And turn round, please.' Again Twinks complied.

There was a long silence, before the Marchioness

pronounced, 'Yes, you look like good breeding stock. You have my permission to marry my son.'

Under other circumstances, Twinks might have responded to this with some passion, pointing out that, when she did finally succumb to marriage, it would be on her terms. But the situation was too urgent for such assertions. 'More important at the moment,' she said, 'is actually finding your son.'

'Oh, indeed. You said you were looking for him.'

'Yes,' said Blotto. 'We saw him last night at a party in the Villa Marzipan.' A sniff of distaste traversed the Marchioness's face as she heard the location. The sniff brought to her nostrils the smell of what in other circumstances she would have sworn was overripe Brie. Now where on earth could that be coming from?

Blotto proceeded to explain about the note they'd received and show it to the old lady. She reacted with fright when she read the contents.

'Do you know La Puce?' asked Twinks.

'I am of course aware of his existence. It is impossible to live on the Riviera without hearing of that monster's evil doings.'

'But you do not know his true identity?'

'Of course not. Nobody knows the true identity of La Puce.'

'Well,' said Blotto, 'We're not going to don the jim-jams at bedtime until we've found out who the stencher is.'

Twinks looked across at her brother with pride. After the uncharacteristic gloom he had shown at the Hôtel Majestic, it was good to see him back as the Blotto she knew and loved, the Blotto who would defy any odds in the cause of decency and justice.

'Anyway,' she said, indicating the note in the Marchioness's claw-like hand, 'your son sent us here because he thought you could help in our search. He says you can put us on the right track. We've established that you don't know the true identity of La Puce, so do you have a mouse-squeak of an idea what he meant?'

The old lady looked thoughtful for a moment. Then she said, 'I really can't think of anything. But then I'm so distraught about this terrible news. The idea that my son is in the clutches of La Puce . . . it's driving every other thought out of my head.'

Her manner did not appear very distraught, but that didn't surprise Blotto and Twinks. They knew what bad form it was for people of their class and nationality to reveal any emotion. So at least the Marchioness of Bluntleigh had learned that much about being an English aristocrat.

'But your son the Marquis must have meant something,' Twinks insisted. 'He was apparently being abducted by La Puce or his acolytes, and he snatched a moment to write a note. Surely, with Wilberforce knows what kind of fate threatening him, whatever he writes in that note must be significant.' The Marchioness agreed. 'So is there anything in there that has a special meaning for you? Some kind of private code your son might use?'

The old lady took her lorgnette back to the note for deeper scrutiny, but eventually confessed with regret that she could not read any private significance into its words.

Twinks took the paper back and focused the full beam of her mighty intellect on the contents. After only a few seconds, she announced, 'Yes, there is something odd here.'

'What?' asked the Marchioness.

'Come on, uncage the ferrets,' said Blotto.

Twinks explained her revelation. 'I think the Marquis wrote this letter with deliberate care, so that if it was intercepted by his captors, La Puce would find out nothing beyond the fact that we were being directed to the Château d'Erimes. But there's something else he's telling us here.'

'What?' repeated the Marchioness.

'Give us the bizz-buzz,' said Blotto.

'Look, the Marquis is an educated man. We know that. He went to Eton.'

The Marchioness nodded confirmation.

Blotto, who was never one to talk up his own intellectual qualities, said, 'Mind you, I went to Eton.'

His sister, choosing not to react to that, went on, 'So one would expect him to write a grammatically correct letter—even at a moment of crisis while being abducted by the acolytes of La Puce.' Another nod from the Marchioness. 'And yet there is one sentence in this note that reads very oddly. Your son tells us that if we come here to visit you, you might be able to send us "down in the right direction and all will be well". Now if he had just written "in the right direction", that would sound better. But no, he says "*down* in the right direction". Does that have any special meaning for you, Lady Bluntleigh?'

For a moment the old lady was silent. Then understanding irradiated her thin face. 'Yes, I have it!'

'Good ticket,' said Blotto.

'My son does not only say "down", he also says that all will be "well". You understand now?'

'No,' said Blotto.

'Yes!' said Twinks. 'He is saying that we should go "down" a "well".'

'Exactly. In the main courtyard here at Château d'Erimes there is a deep well. Tradition and old wives' tales in the village say that the well used to lead to a network of underground tunnels used by smugglers in times gone by.'

'And of course,' Twinks contributed triumphantly, 'La Puce is well known for conducting his business from underground tunnels!'

'Yes,' enthused Blotto. 'You must show us where this well is as quick as a lizard's lick.'

'But no one's been down there for years,' said the Marchioness. 'It will be very dangerous.'

'Larksissimo!' said Twinks.

24

A Secret Passage!

There was an ornamental covering like a small gazebo over the opening of the well in the courtyard of the Château d'Erimes. A brass bucket hung from a rope coiled round a windlass with a handle, but there was not enough on the spool for it to go down very far. The well hadn't been used for a long time; the structure at its head was purely decorative. The Marchioness of Bluntleigh confirmed that when she showed them the entrance.

At least its disuse meant that, as far as Blotto and Twinks could see down, the well was dry. There were also large staples fixed into the circular stone walls in a regular diagonal sequence, clearly intended to be used as steps into the void. How far down that convenient staircase would continue, there was no way of knowing.

The Marchioness, with appropriate lack of emotion, expressed the hope that they would find her son, and Blotto and Twinks assured her that they would. Then the pair hoisted themselves over the edge of the well's lip and started their descent. Hoping that he was now on the way to rescuing Mimsy La Pim, Blotto's derring-do had returned in its full glory and so naturally he went first. Apart from anything else, if one of the staples came loose from the crumbling wall and sent someone down to their death, that someone should definitely be him rather than his sister. The Dowager Duchess still had hopes of breeding from Twinks, after all. And, as a younger son, Blotto had always known he was expendable. His parents had wanted an heir and a spare, and he'd never had any illusions about which role was his.

His only regret, as he set off on the latest stage of their hazardous adventure, was that he couldn't have his trusty cricket bat with him.

Their spiral course downwards on the metal staples was relatively easy, but they were soon beyond the reach of the daylight above. That, however, offered no problem. Twinks produced the electric torch from her infinitely resourceful reticule.

It was difficult for Blotto to judge how far down they were when the staples in the wall ran out. A

180

torchlight recce suggested that they had reached the point where in previous years the well-water had reached. There was a definite line around the walls. A line of dried weed or algae, below which the stone was discoloured to a muddy green. Twinks's torchbeam had insufficient range to reach far into the cylinder of darkness beneath them. Nor did it pick up any reflection from a watery surface, suggesting that the well was, at least as far as they could see, still dry.

'Hm, bit of a tough rusk to chew,' said Blotto after his sweeping free foot had failed to reach any further staples. 'Shall I just shout "By Wilberforce" and jump?'

His sister quickly discouraged such daredevil antics. 'No, Blotters. Even if you only got a broken ankle, that'd put a terrible chock in our cogwheel. We don't know how far you'd fall.'

'But that's what'd make it such beezer fun,' said Blotto, a note of disappointment in his voice.

'No,' said Twinks, with an echo of the Dowager Duchess's tone. 'There'll be plenty of time for heroics once we actually get on to the horizontal plane.'

Blotto took her point on board. 'Tickey-tockey,' he said before, as ever, appealing to his sister's greater intellect. 'So what do we do?'

'We use what I used in Notre-Dame,' said Twinks, reaching once again into her reticule and producing the housewife that contained her spool of extra-strong silk thread. Neatly she hooked the loop round one of the staples, testing the connection for firmness.

'Shall we both pongle on down together?' asked Blotto.

181

'No, don't think so, me old cabbage patch. The silk thread's strong, but I'm not sure it'd take our combined weight. You go first. When you've landed on something solid, give three sharp tugs on the thread.'

'Good ticket,' said Blotto. 'You'd better keep the torch.'

'No. More important you can check out what's down there.'

'Tickey-tockey.'

It was difficult to hold on to something no thicker than button thread, but Blotto improvised a kind of loop around his body and descended in a manner that was almost abseiling.

Twinks, with her feet on one staple and her hands gripping another, watched as the torchlight below dwindled into darkness. Her only comfort was the continuing tautness of the slender silk that supported her brother.

It seemed an age till something happened. First the thread went slack and Twinks nearly panicked that it had broken. But the slackness came gently, rather than suddenly, which reassured her. And then from the depths below she heard a distant cry of 'Hoopee-doopee!', which reassured her even more.

That was quickly followed by the agreed three tugs on the thread, and Twinks started the descent to join her brother.

She found him waiting for her at the opening of a narrow horizontal shaft that led only in one direction from the bottom of the well. Blotto pointed the torch up the well-shaft, highlighting the thin thread of silk down which they had both travelled. 'Pity we can't take that flipmadoodle with us. Might come in handy.'

'I doubt it, Blotters. I think we've nearly got down to sea level. I wouldn't expect any more sharp descents ahead of us. Besides,' she added, 'if we do find Mimsy La Pim, we may well need an escape route to get her back to civilization. We'll be glad we left the thread in position then.'

'Good ticket,' said Blotto.

He then turned the torch on the passage that lay ahead of them. It was clearly a long time since there had been any water in the well. Everything the torchbeam lighted on was dry. Though the walls were discoloured with what had once been slimy weed, that had long browned and was crackly to the touch.

They had to stoop to progress along the passage, and Twinks remembered the detail she had been told by Professor Erasmus Holofernes, that La Puce always recruited midgets for his nefarious schemes. They could run at speed without bending through the sewers that were their boss's favourite working milieu.

'Any idea which direction we're going in?' asked Blotto.

'Towards the sea,' his sister replied immediately.

'How do you know that?'

'I've got a compass in my reticule. I checked it while you were making your way down here.'

'But how could you see it in the dark?'

'It has a luminous needle.'

'You are a Grade A foundation stone,' said Blotto. 'You think of everything.'

As they walked along, uncomfortably crouched, Twinks's words were confirmed by the distinct and increasingly powerful smell of salt water. Not only that, but another, less salubrious odour. Somewhere ahead, their nostrils told them— through the dominant odour of Blotto's sacred Brie—the tunnel they were walking along was going to join up with a system of sewers.

The passage seemed to go on for ever. Each new stretch of the walls revealed by the torchbeam looked exactly like the previous bit. 'I wonder how far we've come,' asked Blotto.

'Thirty-one yards two feet and eight inches vertically down the well,' Twinks replied, 'and four hundred and seventy-three yards one foot and three inches horizontally so far along this passage.'

'Toad-in-the-hole, Twinks! How did you work that out?'

She explained, but her brother got a bit lost in all the details of measuring distances between staples, changes of atmospheric pressure and counting step lengths. Not for the first time Blotto reminded himself that he shouldn't ask Twinks questions like that. No need for explanations. Just listen to whatever she said and assume it was right. Which it always was.

Eventually their torch revealed a variation in the even continuity of the surrounding walls. The unending stone was interrupted by a metal frame set into it. Brother and sister paused when they got there and Twinks ran the torchbeam over the new feature. Closer inspection revealed that the frame was double, forming slots either side and top and bottom.

'What does that brainbox of yours make of this?' asked Blotto.

'I think it's probably some kind of doorway, built on the lines of a portcullis. Big metal shutter comes down, fitting into the slots—and cutting off access from the well.'

'Do you reckon it's still working?'

Twinks drew her torchbeam closer. The metal frame showed a few spots of rust and salt corrosion, but was basically clean. 'Think it could be,' she said.

When they stepped through the portal, they found themselves in a less cramped space where they could both stand up. Though still carved out of the living rock, the passage was a lot bigger, and along one side they saw a row of heavy metal doors with square grilles on them. Out of one of these light trickled.

Blotto moved across to look through the grille. What he saw there brought a surge of elation to his manly bosom.

That elation arose from the fact that, inside the room beyond the grille, he could see Mimsy La Pim. She was strapped to a bed as firmly as she had ever been to a railway line in one of her movies.

'Mimsy!' he cried. 'We are here to rescue you!'

25

Escape?

To Blotto's surprise, when he tried the door handle it yielded immediately to his touch. He found himself in a brightly lit room, whose three facing walls appeared to be made of glass, though through them only darkness was visible.

185

At the sound of the door opening, the trussed-up film star let out a little scream.

'Don't don your worry-boots,' shouted her rescuer. 'It's me, Blotto. And Twinks and me'll have you free in less time than a schoolboy stays in a cold bath.'

'My hero!' said Mimsy La Pim. It was an expression that she had used frequently in her acting career. But this was the first time she'd said it out loud. Normally she mouthed the words and then they appeared on a caption.

Blotto took in how his beloved had been immobilized. The bed on which she lay—and indeed the one beside it—was rather like a hospital trolley, with purpose-built leather straps attached to its sides. These had been firmly buckled round Mimsy's neck, waist, wrists and ankles. And she had been dressed in some kind of hospital gown, as though awaiting an operation. What kind of evil operation that might be, Blotto did not care to contemplate.

As he started the business of releasing his beloved, Blotto asked, 'Who's the stencher who's done this to you?'

'Gee, I think he's someone from Ireland,' replied Mimsy La Pim.

'What makes you think that?' asked Blotto, struggling with the taut leather.

'I was in a movie set in Ireland, and in it someone was stolen away by the "little people" and never seen again. So, because we're so near Ireland, that's what must have happened to me.'

'We're not very near Ireland,' objected Twinks, who had come in to help with the unstrapping process.

'We are too,' said Mimsy. 'We're in France and that's in Europe. So's Ireland. They're both in Europe.'

'Yes, but Europe is quite a big place.'

'It isn't,' Mimsy objected. 'Not compared to the US of A.'

Twinks forbore from taking issue with that assertion. 'Anyway,' she asked, 'what was it you were saying about the "little people"?'

'It was the "little people" who stole me away from the Villa Marzipan. Just like in the movie.'

'Those were not "little people",' said Twinks patiently.

'They were too. They didn't come no higher than my waist. And if that's not little, I'd like to know what is.'

'I meant they were not "little people" in the sense of being leprechauns. They were midgets, employed by La Puce.'

'Oh,' said Mimsy La Pim, taking a moment to try to assimilate this information.

'Anyway,' said Blotto as he loosened the last restraint, 'no time for chittle-chattle. We need to get you out of here.'

'Oh, gee, yes. I've no idea where I am.'

The thought flashed through Twinks's mind that ignorance of where she was was a permanent state with Mimsy La Pim, but she was far too well brought up to voice it. Instead she just said, 'Yes, we'll take you back to the Château d'Erimes.'

'I don't have any shattered dreams,' objected Mimsy. 'I'm American. Americans' dreams always come true.'

Twinks, who was beginning to think that a little of Mimsy La Pim went a long way and that the

187

prospect of having her as a sister-in-law was not an entirely appealing one, said, 'Château d'Erimes is the home of the Marchioness of Bluntleigh.'

'Gee, I thought he was called the Marquis.'

'This is his mother.'

'Wow.'

Mimsy La Pim was now standing up, facing Blotto. The soupiness of their expressions had reached a stage beyond mulligatawny.

'Put a jumping cracker under it!' said Twinks. 'We must get you out of here as soon as possible.' Her brother and his beloved remained transfixed like the two lions over the main gates of Tawcester Towers. 'Move!' his sister commanded and she bustled them out into the passage.

They were just about to go through the metal frame in the direction of the well and the life-saving silk thread, when Blotto stopped. 'We can't go back to the Marchioness like this.'

'What do you mean?' asked his sister.

'Well, we told her we were going down to rescue her son, and we haven't got the Marquis of Bluntleigh with us, have we?'

Mimsy La Pim looked around to be sure. Then she agreed, 'No, we don't.'

Twinks was torn. Part of her reckoned that getting Mimsy to freedom would be achievement enough. But she was also influenced by the long traditions of *noblesse oblige*.

'We'll have to fetch out the poor old greengage,' said Blotto. 'After all, he did go to Eton.'

That clinched it. They would have to go further into the subterranean network of passages to find Buzzer Bluntleigh. They turned back.

Just as they did so, they heard an ominous and

enormous clang from behind them. Blotto and Twinks turned as one to see the last shudder of the metal shutter that had slid down in its slots to cut off their way back to the Château d'Erimes.

Then they heard an evil laugh. It seemed to come from the room from which they had just released Mimsy La Pim. Blotto and Twinks stood on the threshold and looked inside.

The area behind the glass wall was now brightly illuminated, revealing what appeared to be some monstrous laboratory. Tangles of tubing led in every direction. Coloured fluids bubbled unnervingly in retorts. Lights flashed, steam seethed. Midget lab technicians moved busily about, mixing, measuring, monitoring.

And in the centre of this experimentation, dressed in a white coat and laughing at them, stood a figure whose scaly pinkish-brown face tapered down to a sharp-toothed point. Like the face of a flea.

They had finally met La Puce!

26

A Devilish Experiment

'Seize them!' commanded the muffled voice behind the insect face.

As if from nowhere, a gang of midgets in slime-green uniforms appeared and surrounded the three would-be escapees. Blotto managed to send half a dozen of them flying, but without his cricket bat he wasn't at his most effective. Soon the three of them were overwhelmed by sheer weight of numbers.

Once again they heard the evil laugh of La Puce. 'So you walked conveniently into my trap,' he said.

'You mean the Marchioness was part of your plan too?' asked Twinks.

'Of course. For an operation like mine one needs friends in high places.'

'And what in the name of Denzil is your operation?' demanded Blotto. 'What are you hoping to achieve?'

'World domination. Neither more nor less than world domination,' the voice replied in a tone of muffled complacency.

'You have about as much chance of that as a housemaid has of entering the peerage,' said Blotto.

'Don't you believe it. I am well on the way to the realization of my ambitions. And I would like to thank you for your help in getting me nearer that realization.'

'Our help?'

'Your generous donation of the Tawcester Towers' Gainsborough and Reynolds.'

'You four-faced filcher!' cried Twinks. 'So you were behind the theft?'

'Not only that one, but a co-ordinated programme of thefts of Old Masters from all of Europe. It is the sale of those paintings that will finance my successful progress to world domination.'

'But the two Ruperts are our ancestors,' protested Blotto.

'It is not their subjects that give the portraits value,' said La Puce disdainfully. 'It is who painted them that matters. The names of Gainsborough and Reynolds carry far more weight in the world than those of two minor Dukes.'

'*Minor* Dukes?' echoed Blotto. He tried to burst free to attack the lump of toadspawn who could so impugn the Lyminster family honour, but the swarm of uniformed midgets held him firm.

'Yes,' continued the complacent master criminal, 'it is the proceeds from art that will fund my experimentation.'

It was Twinks's turn to do the echoing. 'Experimentation? What kind of murdey game are you up to?'

'A very cunning one,' replied La Puce. 'I have abducted the world's best scientists to work with me on my schemes. The laboratory you see here is just one of many in my underground empire. Nothing can halt the advance of science.'

'Nothing can halt the advance of *good* science,' said Twinks rather magnificently, 'but human beings all over the world can rise up to defeat the advance of *bad* science.'

'I fear not,' said La Puce. 'Because soon there will not be enough human beings in the world to frustrate my plans.'

'What fumacious devilment are you planning?' demanded Blotto.

But his question prompted only another evil laugh and the assertion that: 'You will find out soon enough.' Then La Puce barked out a command to his army of midgets. 'Strap the dark-haired girl back on to her deathbed. And do the same with the man.'

'What about the fair-haired girl?' asked one of the midgets.

'For her a different fate awaits. A much happier fate. I plan to be very generous to the fair-haired girl.'

'I don't want your generosity!' snapped Twinks. 'If Blotto and Mimsy are about to be killed, then I want to share the same fate as them.'

'Ah,' said La Puce. 'Were you not taught by your nanny in the nursery the old adage that "I want never gets"? You may *want* whatever you wish to, Twinks, but the decision about what you actually *get* is mine and mine alone. Strap down the other two!' he commanded the midgets.

Once again no amount of struggling could defeat the numerical supremacy of the midget army. Soon Blotto and Mimsy La Pim were pinioned by the leather straps to their parallel beds, awaiting whatever fate La Puce chose to decree for them.

But Twinks's defiance had not been crushed. 'Your science is useless!' she cried, moving back into magnificent mode. 'It cannot work against the powers of good!'

'Oh no?' La Puce appeared to be amused by her continuing resistance. 'Would you not say that the transformation of my head into that of a giant flea was a triumph of science?'

'No. I would say that was evidence that you purchased a Giant Flea Mask (Product Number 2374J) from Professor Shazamm's Joke and Novelty Shop in London's Charing Cross Road.'

A moment of rather peeved silence told Twinks that she had hit the mark. La Puce did not respond to her accusation, instead changing the subject and shouting, 'Bring the fair-haired one in here . . . while I explain to the other two the fate that awaits them!'

192

Resistance was once again futile as Twinks was frogmarched into the laboratory area and pushed down into a chair to look through the glass at her helpless brother and the equally helpless Mimsy La Pim.

'So let me tell you what is going to happen to these two unfortunates . . .' The muffled voice of La Puce paused, relishing the silence. He was in charge and he was going to reveal his evil machinations at his own pace.

'Now the main problem facing anyone attempting world domination is the sheer number of people in that world. Millions upon millions of them, and each extra million represents an increased problem of control. Therefore the first essential for anyone hoping for world domination is to reduce the number of people he has to control, to reduce the population of the world.

'So if, like me, you have an interest in history, you will ask yourself: What, over the years, has had the greatest effect on world population? War, you might say. Famine. Earthquakes, floods, other natural disasters. But the impact of all of those pales into insignificance when compared to . . . the Plague!

'The Black Death killed a third of the population of Europe, but the Plague that I am developing will make those statistics look paltry. Now I'm sure I don't need to tell you that the bubonic plague is carried by the fleas which infest rats. And let me tell you, down here in my laboratories I have bred a very special kind of rat.'

As he spoke, La Puce flicked a switch and light appeared behind the two glass side walls of Blotto and Mimsy's prison. It took a moment for them and Twinks to register that the seething mass of grey and pink thus revealed was in fact individual rats, crawling over each other and baring their yellowed teeth against the restraint of the glass. With realization of what they were came recognition of the fact that they were not ordinary rats. They were super-rats, the smallest of which was the size of a badger.

Before they had time to put on their brave faces, Blotto and Twinks's eyes registered terror. Mimsy La Pim didn't bother with putting on a brave face; she stayed with the expression of terror.

La Puce laughed at their discomfiture. 'Yes, and of course if the rats are that big, imagine the size of the fleas on them! Imagine the effects of a bite from such a flea! But no, you will not have to imagine. I would not put you to so much trouble. I will instead arrange a demonstration for you. It is the demonstration I had planned to use Mimsy La Pim for, but now I am fortunate to have a second . . . what shall I call it . . . guinea pig? Now I will be able to monitor the symptoms of bubonic plague on both the female and male body!'

He waved to his green-uniformed midget army. 'Clear the room . . . unless you too wish to be part of my experiment.'

His acolytes needed no second invitation. Falling over themselves in a manner not dissimilar to the giant rats, they scuttled out into the corridor, locking the prison door behind them.

Twinks looked contemptuously at their tormentor. 'You'll never get away with this, you stencher!' she said.

La Puce chuckled again. 'But I have already got away with it, the important part, anyway. There

194

are just a few more details that I need to sort out, and then I will unleash my particularly fatal strain of bubonic plague on to the unsuspecting world!'

'If that's what you're planning, then the least you can do is let me through into the room, so that my brother and I can die together.'

The insect head shook. 'No, no. I know a little of how cunning you are, Twinks. If I let you join Blotto, you might devise some scheme to thwart my ambitions. Besides,' he went on, the muffled voice taking on an even more sinister tone, 'I do not wish you to die in there, Twinks. I have other plans for you.'

'If you think I am going to fit in with any plans of yours, then—'

'Silence her!' shouted La Puce, and four midget lab technicians came forward to do as he told them. 'You know where to take her.'

Gagged and helpless, Twinks was dragged out of the laboratory, out of sight of her brother and Mimsy La Pim.

'Now,' said La Puce, 'I think it is time for you two and my super-rats to get better acquainted.'

As he spoke, he pressed a switch and, in pure synchronicity, the two glass walls either side of the prison were raised, allowing the super-rats to burst in and swarm over everything inside the room.

Including the beds on which lay the immobilized bodies of Blotto and Mimsy La Pim.

La Puce then departed his observation room, returning it to its former darkness. The echo of his evil laugh lingered in his wake.

27

A Fate Worse Than Death

Though none of her abductors reached higher than her waist, Twinks was not strong enough to resist them. Two midgets clung on to each of her wrists, while the bulk of them pushed from behind. One, whose uniform boasted more decoration than the others, strode ahead to open the doors.

And there were a lot of doors. As she was hustled through, Twinks began to get some concept of the scale of La Puce's operation. Laboratory opened out into laboratory and in none of them did the tiny white-coated technicians look up from their work for a moment at the strange cavalcade. In some of the laboratories chemical experiments bubbled and fizzed; in others, sparks and blazes of electricity zapped between pieces of apparatus; in some, caged rats of various sizes were being tested and vivisected. And through the glass walls of each laboratory they crossed were revealed other laboratories, stretching away as far as the eye could see.

Eventually the laboratories gave way to a lavish living area, a kind of mansion carved out of the living rock. Twinks was escorted through a cavernous hallway. Doors they passed opened out to luxuriously appointed drawing rooms, but the relentless onward pushing of her midget guards showed they hadn't yet reached their destination.

The room where they did finally stop was much more primitive. A circular space like a cell, its walls were bare, clean rock. Opposite the door through which they entered was a substantial closed one, its strong oak panels studded with metal bosses in the shape of fleurs-de-lys.

There was no furniture or adornment of any kind. Except for a large bouquet of flowers standing in an otherwise empty glass vase. And, hanging from a rivet driven into the wall, a beautiful white wedding dress.

The midget with the more decorated uniform ordered Twinks to put it on.

At first she resisted, but it soon became clear that if she didn't undress herself her captors would do the job for her. So, commanding them to stand back, Twinks proceeded to change into the dress.

She had no prudery about revealing her undergarments. The midget army of La Puce became as invisible to her as any of the Tawcester Towers domestics.

Two things struck her as she donned the white dress. First, that it was a beautiful garment, made from the finest materials by the finest seamstresses. And second, that it fitted her so perfectly that she could have been measured for it.

When she had completed dressing, the senior midget thrust the bouquet towards her. She took it with her left hand, making sure to keep her reticule in her right. Then the midget moved across and turned the heavy ring handle on the studded door.

It opened to reveal a small but exquisitely beautiful candlelit chapel. The splendour of its altar and the excesses of its statuary suggested it was a Catholic chapel, and this was confirmed by the smell of incense that emanated from the interior.

Standing in front of the altar was a priest in elaborate robes and a black biretta.

'Welcome,' he said in English. 'Welcome, you who are about to become the bride of La Puce.'

28

The Plague!

On very rare occasions Blotto had really good ideas. They were always of a practical nature, never flights of intellectual fancy. And fortunately he'd had one of his good ideas when he was being pinioned to his hospital trolley by the midget army. He had taken the sensible precaution of unbuckling the strap of his wristwatch and ensuring that the leather restraint was pulled tight over that part of his wrist. By flexing the muscles of his arm he had eased the wristwatch off, thus rendering his leather ligature loose enough for him to slip out his hand.

And for the first time in Blotto's life, a second good idea followed hard on the heels of the first one. In the seconds before he was swamped by super-rats, he reached into his blazer pocket and produced his sacred relic, the Brie that Mimsy La Pim had been eating at the Villa Marzipan. Deftly, he smeared it over the other leather straps that bound him.

Now the fondness of rodents for cheese is proverbial and extolled the world over by manufacturers of mousetraps. So, offered the choice of fresh young human bodies and overripe Brie, La Puce's super-rats had no hesitation. Their mouths reached for the precious flavour and their sharp teeth tore through the leather straps impregnated with it.

Within seconds Blotto was free! Once again he thought wistfully of what he could have done with his cricket bat in his hand . . . Still, it wasn't the moment for regrets. He'd have to make do with whatever weapons were to hand. Grabbing the tail of a particularly large rat, he whirled it round his head with his left hand, sending other rats smashing against the glass walls of the cell. Meanwhile, with his right hand he unbuckled the restraints that tied Mimsy La Pim to her bed.

In a moment she too was free! Not waiting for a caption, again she breathed the words: 'My hero!'

They had seen no exit from their cell into La Puce's observation room, but through the grille of the door by which they'd entered, a thin light challenged the darkness. Fortunately, the midget army had not locked up after them, so within moments Blotto and Mimsy La Pim were out in the passage.

The film star had never seen anyone as handsome as Blotto at that moment. His blue eyes sparkling with honesty and chivalry, he cried out: 'Come on, we must shift like a pair of cheetahs on spikes and rescue Twinks!'

29

A Villain Unmasked!

'You will wait here,' commanded the priest, 'until we are joined by the man you are to marry.'

Twinks had no option but to obey. She was held tight by the midget army in her position before the altar.

Though matrimony was not the preoccupation with her that it was for most girls of her age, even Twinks had from time to time pictured the day of her wedding. But none of the images she had entertained bore any relation to the situation in which she now found herself. They hadn't included a Catholic priest, or an army of midgets, or indeed a chapel hollowed out of rocks in the South of France. And they certainly hadn't included, in the role of groom, a criminal mastermind disguised as a giant flea.

Twinks focused her mind on her reticule. There must be something amid its inexhaustible supplies that could help in her current predicament. But as she itemized the contents, none of them seemed to offer any escape from her approaching fate.

She looked around the chapel and saw something that brought a new chill to her heart. Across the altar, displayed like the colours of some vanquished army, lay her brother's cricket bat!

Now she knew the full perfidy of the stenchers they were up against.

Twinks tried to engage the priest in conversation. 'Even if you do go through the mockery of a wedding service with me and La Puce, it will not be legal without my voicing my consent. And I'll have my tongue pulled out with red-hot pliers before I give that consent!'

'The marriage will be legal,' said the priest complacently. 'There will be enough witnesses here who will all swear blind that they heard you give your consent. Won't there?'

The midget army confirmed that they would act as witnesses.

'So you will be married,' said the priest. 'And I don't know why you're making such a fuss about the idea. There are many women whose cherished dream it would be to marry the most powerful man in the world.'

'Well, I'm not one of those women!' came the spirited response. 'When I get married, it will be to someone of my choosing.' For that moment she put from her mind any influence her mother the Dowager Duchess might have on such decisions. 'I don't consort with criminals!'

'Criminals,' said a muffled voice behind her, 'are only defined by the laws they break. When I rule the world, I will define what is against the law. And I can assure you that, by that definition, I will never have committed a criminal act.'

The restraining midgets relaxed their grip sufficiently for Twinks to turn and face her nemesis. La Puce had removed his white laboratory coat and was dressed in immaculate morning dress. Just like a proper bridegroom.

'I will never marry you!' cried Twinks magnificently.

'Oh, but you will. You have no choice,' said the muffled voice silkily. 'And after a time you will

201

begin to understand the benefits of our union. As the bubonic plague from my super-rats decimates the world's population, you will come to realize how safe you are in my protective arms.'

'Never!' cried Twinks, with the bold certainty of one of Mimsy La Pim's caption cards.

'Oh yes,' said La Puce. 'You will be the perfect consort for me. Together we will rule the world! And now . . .' he continued as he stepped forward, 'let the wedding service begin.'

The priest's mouth was opened, but before any sacred words could emerge from it, a breathless midget appeared at the entrance of the chapel, crying, 'The rats have all escaped! They are running down the passage that opens out by the sea!'

This news did not seem to discomfit La Puce much. Calmly he said, 'I do not wish them to go out into the world yet. I have planned their release for two days hence, and I never change my plans. Don't worry, I will seal off the end of the tunnel and they can be herded back into their cells.'

Reaching forward, La Puce took hold of one of the candlesticks on the altar and pulled it towards him. It was hinged like a lever and as he pulled, a distant sound of chains clanking and machinery whirring was heard. Letting go of the candlestick, he announced, 'There, it is done. The metal shutter at the sea end of the tunnel is closed and the rats are trapped between that and the shutter which cuts off access to the Château d'Erimes.'

He turned to the midget who had just bought the news of their escape. 'You and your men can get them back into their cells.'

'I am not sure we can do that, La Puce. The rats

202

are very dangerous and are likely to turn on us and—'

'Get them back into their cells!'

More frightened by the wrath of his boss than the viciousness of the rats, the midget rushed off to obey the bellowed command.

When La Puce next spoke, his voice was all insinuating intimacy. 'And now let us return to the wedding service. This is a moment I have yearned for for a long time. A great moment—and an appropriate one—when the Honourable Honoria Lyminster, the most beautiful and intelligent woman in the world, is united for ever to the most powerful man in the world. Father, let the wedding service commence!'

And so it did. Pinioned as she was, Twinks could only listen as the liturgical process unrolled. When it came to responding to the three questions in the Rite of Marriage about the freedom of her choice, her faithfulness to her husband and her intention to bring up her children in the Catholic faith, she kept her mouth firmly shut. But on each occasion, behind her she heard the massed voices of the midgets saying in unison, 'Yes, we heard her answer.'

When it came to the moment for the ring to be placed on her finger, La Puce gestured to the midget guards to release Twinks's left arm. She wasn't going to waste an opportunity like that. In a movement almost too fast to be seen, she grabbed the pointed end of La Puce's mask and whipped it off his face.

She looked inside it and triumphantly read what was written on a small label there. 'See, I knew I was right. It's a Giant Flea Mask (Product Number

2374J) from Professor Shazamm's Joke and Novelty Shop in London's Charing Cross Road!'

Then she looked up into the eyes of the Marquis of Bluntleigh.

30

The Rodents' Revenge

'You!' said Twinks in a voice of ice-cold fury. 'You were behind the whole thing.'

'Yes,' said Buzzer Bluntleigh with a sardonic smile.

'But why? Why did you go through all that flip-madoodle of pretending to be an amorous swain?'

'Because I was an amorous swain. I've been in love since I first clapped my peepers on you, Twinks.'

She was so used to receiving protestations of this kind that she hardly even heard it. 'But why go through all that chivalry rombooley, all that mooning and mawking, writing terrible poems—?'

'They weren't terrible poems,' said the Marquis, offended.

'Yes, they were. Total bilge-water.'

'But I thought—'

'Anyway, why go through all that when, as you've just proved, you could capture me by force?'

'Because I *am* chivalrous, Twinks. I was brought up to do things the right way. I went to Eton, after all. And I wanted you to become my wife in the proper way, with the full agreement of your family. It was only when I finally recognized that was never going to happen that I resorted to force.'

'But all that pathetic guff, drooping around like a lovesick lily. What did you think you'd achieve by all that?'

'I thought it was the way to your heart.'

'Well, it wasn't, by Denzil! And believe me, none of it has done you a groatsworth of good. I'll never marry you.'

'I think technically,' said the priest, 'you just have married him.'

'Don't talk such toffee! I never gave my consent to anything!'

'Oh yes, you did,' intoned the midget army. 'We heard you. You're married all right.'

'And in a moment,' said the Marquis of Bluntleigh, 'you will have my ring on your finger.'

'Never!'

But despite her protestations, Twinks was not strong enough to resist. Midget hands seized her left hand and forced it up towards the waiting gold band. Flesh and precious metal had almost made contact when a voice behind them was heard to say, 'Hello, Twinks me old buttered muffin, what's the bizz-buzz?'

Bride and groom turned together at the sound to see Blotto and Mimsy La Pim, both grinning hugely.

'Beezer to find you, Twinks! And you, Buzzer. Beezer to see you too!' Blotto moved forward to take the Marquis by the hand. The Marquis smiled back. 'I was afraid my sister had fallen into the clutches of La Puce.'

'He *is* La Puce!' hissed Twinks.

'Don't talk such guff!' said her brother. 'He went to Eton. Boddos who go to Eton don't disguise themselves as Giant Fleas and become criminal masterminds.'

'No, of course we don't,' Buzzer Bluntleigh agreed.

'Yes, they do!' Twinks's quick mind thought of the one thing that would convince Blotto of the Marquis's villainy. 'Look at what's on the altar!'

She'd made the right call. With a cry of 'You were the stencher who snaffled it!', Blotto seized his cricket bat and turned on its purloiner.

Mimsy La Pim looked at the bat in puzzlement. 'Gee, what's that?' she asked.

But Blotto was too incensed to provide her with an immediate answer. Instead, he shouted at Buzzer Bluntleigh, 'You lump of toadspawn! Anyone who steals another boddo's cricket bat instantly gives up all rights to the title of Old Etonian!'

The smile evaporated from the Marquis of Bluntleigh's face and he shouted to his midget army, 'Seize them!'

The little men ran forward, but they were no match for a Blotto armed with his cricket bat and an unassailable sense of his own righteousness. Using the full repertory of strokes that had brought him such glory on the playing fields of Eton, he belaboured the approaching midgets and soon had them on the back foot. They were quickly joined by the Marquis of Bluntleigh as, in the face of the flailing cricket bat, their progress turned to a rout.

Twinks and Mimsy La Pim followed behind Blotto, watching his feats with matching adoration.

Back through the living quarters La Puce's army was driven, and back through the maze of

206

laboratories. Midgets slipped and stumbled against each other, getting bruised and battered in the confusion of their retreat. Eventually the army and their leader escaped from the clubbing cricket bat into the passage that ran from the closed Château d'Erimes exit to the closed seashore exit.

And there in the passage they encountered the super-sized rodents created by the evil experiments of La Puce. Now a cornered rat is proverbially vicious and the super-rats, having found both ends of the tunnel sealed, felt decidedly cornered. Their animal instincts left them no alternative but to turn on the people whom they blamed for that cornering.

The Marquis of Bluntleigh and his midget army stood no chance against the ravening horde of rats.

Behind the safety of a glass wall Twinks decided that, if she had actually been married, then she'd been so quickly widowed that it would never be worth mentioning the fact to anyone.

31

The Proper Authorities

Careful exploration of the network of La Puce's laboratories was a rather bizarre experience. Blotto and Twinks had been worried that, though the uniformed army of midgets had been neutralized by the super-rats, the research team of white-coated ones might turn on them. But as brother and sister moved from the scene of one ghastly experiment to another, none of the staff so much as looked up to acknowledge their presence. The midget researchers had been conditioned through some evil system of brain manipulation to focus all of their concentration on furthering La Puce's evil ambitions.

This was of course good news for Blotto and Twinks and enabled them to conduct their searches without anxiety. Stowed away in the subterranean labyrinth they found many unexpected objects, including neatly folded hot-air balloons, which explained how the Gainsborough and Reynolds had been spirited away from the top of Notre-Dame.

They also found files full of personnel records of La Puce's network of international art thieves. The Vicomte and Vicomtesse de Sales-Malincourt (whose real names turned out to be the rather more prosaic Thierry and Marie Dupont) of course featured in these documents, but they were only two among many and the aristocratic sleuths began to comprehend the scope of La Puce's operations.

In the files Blotto and Twinks found paperwork that revealed what had happened with the booby-trap in Notre-Dame. They had misunderstood the message received at the Hôtel de Crillon. Blotto had been the one intended to go to the South Tower. La Puce had never wanted to eliminate the woman he planned to marry. Blotto was the one intended to step on the sabotaged trapdoor. Had he done so, of course, not being in possession of a reticule containing a housewife and extra-strong silken thread, he would have plummeted to his death.

The most important of their discoveries, though,

was made in a high warehouse hollowed out of the rock, where they found a treasure trove of Old Masters, the loot from almost every major art theft of the past decade. Address tickets and dates on the frames of the works showed that they were all due to be delivered to their illicit buyers on the following day. They had stopped La Puce's wicked plans just in time. Backed up by the money from the sales of those paintings, and with his packs of plague-bearing super-rats ready to be unleashed, nothing could have obstructed his plans for world domination.

And, joyfully, among the stacks of incalculably valuable artworks, Blotto and Twinks found the objects of their quest, the two Ruperts. Leaving all the other paintings where they were, they reclaimed the Gainsborough and Reynolds and looked forward to rehanging them in their proper place, the Long Gallery of Tawcester Towers.

As soon as they got back to the Hôtel Majestic, Twinks began the task that she always took upon herself at this stage in one of their investigations. She wrote up a dossier of the devilment they had uncovered, detailing all the crimes of La Puce and exposing his real identity as the Marquis of Bluntleigh. She also pointed to the probable guilt of his mother the Marchioness, who must have been primed to direct Blotto and Twinks down the well into what was meant to be a fatal trap.

Because of their location, Twinks wrote up her dossier in fluent French. She was awake all night finishing it, and in the morning instructed Corky Froggett to deliver the large folder to the office of the local *gendarmerie*.

Whether its findings would be acted upon, or

whether the local police chief had really been bought off by La Puce, was not her concern. Twinks had once again done her duty by passing the information on to the proper authorities.

And if those authorities wanted to take credit for the success of the investigation, they would hear no objections from her.

32

Fairytale Ending

They had all arranged to meet at the Café Floure, where it was still warm enough to sit outside. Blotto and Twinks were there first and after the briefest of commentaries on Hobbes's mechanistic view of the Social Contract, the waiter departed to fetch the coffees they ordered. Blotto went off to use the toilet facilities which, like the ones Corky had described in Paris, were of the 'Crouch and Hope' variety.

From inside his cubicle he heard the approach of two voices, which he quickly identified as those of Eugène Blocque and Gaston Tacquelle. Though they were speaking mostly French, he did catch enough sentences in English to deduce that the two painters had been to see Dr Cooper, the English chest specialist recommended by Derek Gringe. And they hadn't liked what he had told them.

' "Just a cold"!' Blocque quoted contemptuously. '*Le salaud!*'

Blotto just managed to restrain himself from

saying, 'Hello.'

'*Moi aussi.* "Just a cold"!' Tacquelle quoted with matching contempt.

'*Mais c'est la phtisie!*'

'*C'est vrai. C'est la phtisie!*'

'*Et cet idiot anglais,* Dr Cooper, *a dit . . .*' Eugène Blocque went into a diminishing impersonation of the chest specialist. ' "Take this medicine twice a day and everything will have cleared up within a week." *Pouf!*' said Eugène Blocque.

'*Pouf!*' Gaston Tacquelle agreed.

' "This medicine"—*pouf*!' said Eugène Blocque.

Blotto heard the sound of a bottle being uncorked and its contents being poured down a urinal.

' "This medicine"—*pouf*!' said Gaston Tacquelle.

Blotto heard the same sequence of sound effects repeated.

'*Je suis malade de la phtisie,*' said Eugène Blocque proudly, his voice fading away as he left the facilities.

'*Moi aussi,*' asserted Gaston Tacquelle proudly, his voice also fading. '*Je suis malade de la phtisie.*'

And they embarked on a fading polyphony of coughing.

*   *   *

By the time Blotto went out to join Twinks, the table had filled up. Blocque and Tacquelle were there, still coughing. Chuck Waggen and Scott Frea had also appeared. And so had Giles Strappe-Cash, whose first words to his distant cousin were, 'Hello. Could you lend me a fiver?'

As he sat down, Blotto handed the note across. A

look at his sister told him that she was getting rather bored by the conversation around her.

It focused, of course, on her beauty.

'You must come back to Paris with me,' Eugène Blocque was saying once again. 'I will immortalize you as the *chef d'oeuvre* of *Triangulisme*.'

'No, no,' Gaston Tacquelle protested. 'You must stay down here with me. It is I who will make you the *chef d'oeuvre* of *Triangulisme*.'

The two artists got into an argument so intense that they both forgot to cough.

Twinks looked wearily across at her brother. From her expression Blotto detected that, whatever vanity she had once entertained about the idea of being immortalized as a painter's muse, it was rapidly evaporating.

Nor did she seem much keener on the idea of becoming a writer's muse either. Her eyes were glazing over as she listened to the two Americans.

'I'll make you famous. For all posterity. Not only in my books. The books I write,' Chuck Waggen was saying, 'but also in all the biographies. Biographies of me. You'll be in all of them.'

'And in mine,' said Scott Frea. 'I'll make you famous. You'll feature in all the biographies of me too.'

'I'll bet there'll be more biographies of me than there are of you,' said Chuck Waggen.

'No, there will be more of me,' said Scott Frea.

And, like the two painters, the two writers started bickering with each other.

Blotto looked at Twinks, who with a little jerk of her head conveyed the 'let's get the hell out of here' message. He nodded.

The two writers and the two painters were far

too preoccupied by their arguments to notice Blotto and Twinks's departure. Giles Strappe-Cash might have spoiled everything by drawing attention to them, but the couple of fivers thrust into his hands by Blotto bought his silence.

The two aristocratic sleuths crept away on tiptoe to where the Lagonda and its patient chauffeur waited.

'Full throttle, Corky!' cried Twinks. 'Back to the Hôtel Majestic and we'll leave as soon as our bags have been packed—and we've got the Gainsborough and the Reynolds safely stowed. Oh, and as soon as I've sent a cablegram.'

'To whom?' asked her brother.

'Dimpsy Wickett-Coote. I'm going to tell her the field is hers. Once Blocque and Tacquelle and Chuck and Scott are in Paris again, it won't take them long to get back to the idea that she's the most beautiful woman in the world. She can be made famous as the *chef d'oeuvre* of *Triangulisme*. And I . . .' Twinks hugged herself in relief, 'will be shot of the lot of them.'

'So once you've done the cablegram, milady,' asked Corky Froggett, 'it'll be full speed back to Tawcester Towers, will it?'

'It certainly will. Home in time for Christmas—larksissimo!' Twinks was surprised to see a shade of melancholy in her brother's expression. 'What's up, Blotto me old clothes-brush? What's pulled your face down?'

In a sombre tone he replied, 'There's just something I must do before I go back to Tawcester Towers.'

*   *   *

Blotto and Mimsy La Pim stood on a terrace of the Hôtel Majestic, enjoying the view of the Mediterranean and the surprisingly mild December evening air. She was once again dressed in black and white and carried a black handbag, but her lips were once again a luscious red.

'Gee, Blotto,' she murmured. 'You were so brave when you defeated La Puce.'

'Oh, don't talk such toffee,' he said, as ever embarrassed by compliment. There was a silence. Blotto's Adam's apple bobbled like a balloon caught in a high wind. Then he said, 'Erm . . .'

'Erm what?' asked Mimsy.

'Just erm . . .' he said.

'I'm so glad we met,' said Mimsy.

Blotto agreed that he was very glad they'd met, too.

'Otherwise we wouldn't be here now talking,' said Mimsy.

'No . . . Well, I suppose it's just possible . . . you know, that we might have bumped into each other this evening just by chance, both being in the same hotel and . . . but that chance is a hundred-to-one outsider. No, it's more likely that we'd be here talking if we had already met and made an arrangement to meet again this evening.'

'Like we did.'

'Yes.'

Another silence ensued. Blotto's Adam's apple bobbled like a tennis ball going over a weir.

'Gee,' said Mimsy, 'we don't have a lot to say to each other, do we?'

'No.'

'Though there's a lot I want to say to you.'

'There's a lot I want to say to you too, Mimsy. But I can't find the words.'

'Gee, I hope you do find them. It's not easy talking without words.'

'No, they are essential.'

'They sure are. Except in movies, of course.'

'Except in movies.' Another silence stretched between them. 'I'll never meet anyone like you again, Mimsy.'

'Well, you might.'

'How?'

'Well, if you met me again. I'm like me. In fact I'm more like me than anyone else you might meet.'

'Good ticket,' said Blotto, and was once again silent.

Mimsy La Pim helped him out. 'What you're saying, Blotto, is that we're not going to meet again, aren't you?'

He nodded miserably. 'You've felt it too, haven't you?'

She sighed. 'Yes.'

'There are just too many differences between us.'

'I know. You've got a title and I'm just plain old Pookie Klunch from Idaho.'

'That's not it!' Blotto protested. 'I wouldn't let something like that get in our way. I'd marry you if you'd been brought up in a pigsty.'

'I was, actually,' said Mimsy La Pim. 'There wasn't too much room in the farmhouse.'

'But . . .' Blotto gulped. The words just wouldn't come.

Again Mimsy helped him out. 'But we're not talking about marriage, are we?'

Blotto shook his head sadly. 'No.' A silence.

'When did you realize it, Mimsy?'

'I think I knew when you said no wife of yours could ever have a job.'

'Oh?'

'I love my work. I love making movies. I couldn't stop doing it.'

'Ah.' There was a wealth of meaning in that monosyllable. It encompassed all of Blotto's upbringing, everything he'd ever been taught to believe in, and—most of all—the thought of the Dowager Duchess's reaction to his marrying a film actress. The code of *noblesse oblige* could sometimes be cruel.

'And when did you know, Blotto?'

'Oh, I've known myself most of my life, really.'

'No. When did you know—pause—Blotto? When did you know that we couldn't get married?'

'I'm afraid it was in the chapel.'

'Gee, you mean when you confronted La Puce?'

'Just before that. When I reclaimed my cricket bat . . . and you saw it and . . .' The words were dried up by the strength of his emotions.

'And what, Blotto?'

'And you didn't know what it was. Broken biscuits, I thought. I am actually in the same room as a poor thimble who doesn't know what a cricket bat is. And that became a . . . oh, what's the word . . . one of those things you bash with a stick.'

'A servant?'

'No, a cymbal, that's it. The fact that you didn't know what a cricket bat was became a symbol of the vast difference between us.'

'Yes, Blotto. I knew it too.'

The silence that followed this was huge, all-encompassing. Blotto's honest blue eyes gazed hopelessly into Mimsy's black ones. Hers filled with tears.

Bereft of words, Mimsy La Pim reached into her handbag. She pulled out a decoratively bordered caption and held it up to Blotto. It read: 'I WILL NEVER FORGET YOU.'

* * *

Brother and sister were back in Tawcester Towers well in time for Christmas. For a few days Blotto moped around, coming to terms with the idea that he'd met a woman who had very nearly meant as much to him as his cricket bat.

But he wasn't very good at being miserable, least of all back on his home ground. He comforted himself with the thought that he could pick up his old habit of going to the cinematograph. There he could sympathize with Mimsy La Pim's latest problem, being swapped at birth for another baby or whatever it might be. He could rail against the moustache-twirling villains who kept tying her to the railway lines. And he could share with her a relationship that was much purer and easier than the kind that involves spending lots of time together.

So by Boxing Day—and particularly by the time of the Boxing Day Hunt, when he felt the massive power of Mephistopheles between his thighs as they tore great holes out of the local farmers' fields, the barometer needle of Blotto's disposition had returned to its habitual setting of 'Sunny'.

```
1    2    3    4    5    6    7    8    9    10    11   12   13   14   15
16   17   18   19   20   21   22   23   24   25    26   27   28   29   30
31   32   33   34   35   36   37   38   39   40    41   42   43   44   45
46   47   48   49   50   51   52   53   54   55    56   57   58   59   60
61   62   63   64   65   66   67   68   69   70    71   72   73   74   75
76   77   78   79   80   81   82   83   84   85    86   87   88   89   90
91   92   93   94   95   96   97   98   99   100

101  102  103  104  105  106  107  108  109  110   111  112  113  114  115
116  117  118  119  120  121  122  123  124  125   126  127  128  129  130
131  132  133  134  135  136  137  138  139  140   141  142  143  144  145
146  147  148  149  150  151  152  153  154  155   156  157  158  159  160
161  162  163  164  165  166  167  168  169  170   171  172  173  174  175
176  177  178  179  180  181  182  183  184  185   186  187  188  189  190
191  192  193  194  195  196  197  198  199  200

201  202  203  204  205  206  207  208  209  210   211  212  213  214  215
216  217  218  219  220  221  222  223  224  225   226  227  228  229  230
231  232  233  234  235  236  237  238  239  240   241  242  243  244  245
246  247  248  249  250  251  252  253  254  255   256  257  258  259  260
261  262  263  264  265  266  267  268  269  270   271  272  273  274  275
276  277  278  279  280  281  282  283  284  285   286  287  288  289  290
291  292  293  294  295  296  297  298  299  300

301  302  303  304  305  306  307  308  309  310   311  312  313  314  315
316  317  318  319  320  321  322  323  324  325   326  327  328  329  330
331  332  333  334  335  336  337  338  339  340   341  342  343  344  345
346  347  348  349  350  351  352  353  354  355   356  357  358  359  360
361  362  363  364  365  366  367  368  369  370   371  372  373  374  375
376  377  378  379  380  381  382  383  384  385   386  387  388  389  390
391  392  393  394  395  396  397  398  399  400

401  402  403  404  405  406  407  408  409  410   411  412  413  414  415
416  417  418  419  420  421  422  423  424  425   426  427  428  429  430
431  432  433  434  435  436  437  438  439  440   441  442  443  444  445
446  447  448  449  450  451  452  453  454  455   456  457  458  459  460
461  462  463  464  465  466  467  468  469  470   471  472  473  474  475
476  477  478  479  480  481  482  483  484  485   486  487  488  489  490
491  492  493  494  495  496  497  498  499  500
```

M/c 3209 | 0 50